"So your kind of man doesn't have to leap from burning cars, tunnel under mountains or drive motorcycles off cliffs?"

"Nah, I prefer a man who is a little more…subtle about his masculinity." Jenna smiled up at Grant. It had been a long time since she had flirted with someone.

"My kind of hero can make dinner, sweep the floor and help children do homework, all at the same time," she said.

Grant halted on the sidewalk and turned to face her. "Well then, hey." He lifted his hands, palms up. "I can do all of that and then some."

"I know you can." She glanced at him, suddenly feeling shy. "I'm sorry, Grant," she said, avoiding his smoldering gaze. "I didn't mean to—"

To her surprise, he caught both of her hands and gently pulled her toward him, their bodies almost touching.

"Jenna," he whispered, as he completed the motion and drew her into full contact against his warm, strong chest. "I want to kiss you…."

Dear Reader,

Brr… February's below-freezing temperatures call for a mug of hot chocolate, a fuzzy afghan and a heartwarming book from Silhouette Romance. Our books will heat you to the tips of your toes with the sizzling sexual tension that courses between our stubborn heroes and the determined heroines who ultimately melt their hardened hearts.

In Judy Christenberry's *Least Likely To Wed,* her sinfully sexy cowboy hero has his plans for lifelong bachelorhood foiled by the searing kisses of a spirited single mom. While in Sue Swift's *The Ranger & the Rescue,* an amnesiac cowboy stakes a claim on the heart of a flame-haired heroine—but will the fires of passion still burn when he regains his memory?

Tensions reach the boiling point in Raye Morgan's *She's Having My Baby!*—the final installment of the miniseries HAVING THE BOSS'S BABY—when our heroine discovers just who fathered her baby-to-be.... And tempers flare in Rebecca Russell's *Right Where He Belongs,* in which our handsome hero must choose between his cold plan for revenge and a woman's warm and tender love.

Then simmer down with the incredibly romantic heroes in Teresa Southwick's *What If We Fall In Love?* and Colleen Faulkner's *A Shocking Request.* You'll laugh, you'll cry, you'll fall in love all over again with these deeply touching stories about widowers who get a second chance at love.

So this February, come in from the cold and warm your heart and spirit with one of these temperature-raising books from Silhouette Romance. Don't forget the marshmallows!

Happy reading!

Mary-Theresa Hussey

Mary-Theresa Hussey
Senior Editor

A Shocking Request

COLLEEN FAULKNER

Published by Silhouette Books
America's Publisher of Contemporary Romance

For Donna Clayton.
Thanks for being so willing to slide over on the bench.
You're a true friend.

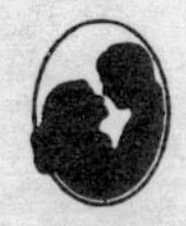

SILHOUETTE BOOKS

ISBN 0-373-19573-7

A SHOCKING REQUEST

This edition published by arrangement with Harlequin Books S.A.

Visit Silhouette at www.eHarlequin.com

Printed in U.S.A.

COLLEEN FAULKNER

had romance writing encrypted in her genetic code. Her mother, Judith E. French, is also a bestselling historical romance author. Whether through genes or simply karma, Colleen began her writing career early. She published her first historical romance at the tender age of twenty-four. Since then she has sold twenty-three historical romance novels, five contemporary romances and six novellas.

Colleen resides in southern Delaware with her husband of twenty years, the couple's four children, a Bernese mountain dog named Duncan and a Siamese cat named Xena. When she's not writing, Colleen enjoys playing racquetball and volleyball, coaching girls' softball and coed soccer and, of course, reading.

Dear Reader,

I can't tell you how excited I am to be publishing my first Silhouette Romance novel. In the last fifteen years, I've written two dozen historical romances, so writing a modern-day love story was quite a challenge. In writing *A Shocking Request*, if there's one thing I learned, it's that romance and love are the same no matter where in time they take place.

A Shocking Request came about when a group of friends and I were talking over coffee about our families and what we would do if we discovered we were dying. All of us realized we would be concerned not just for our children, but for our husbands, too. We all agreed that, out of love, we would want to give our spouses permission to date, fall in love and marry again. Laughing, we agreed we would like to pick out the perfect woman to mother our children and love the man we loved. Some may think that *A Shocking Request* is a sad story, but it's not. It's a story of joy. It's the story of a man and woman who find love after great loss and proves to us once again that love really can conquer all.

Colleen Faulkner

Chapter One

"Happy anniversary, Happy anniversary, Happy anniversary...Happy...Happy...Happy," Grant sang aloud to himself. He had no idea when he had heard the tune, but knew it was from a Flintstones cartoon. He tapped his foot as he waited for the noodles to boil and when they were done, he drained them in the sink. A little milk, a little margarine, that yellow packet of powder that was supposed to be cheese, and voilà, he had an anniversary dinner fit for a...

Fit for a widower on his wedding anniversary, he thought as he dumped the entire pot of macaroni and cheese into a big chili bowl. He grabbed a spoon and the glass of Chardonnay he had poured himself and carried it into the den, shutting off the lights behind him. In the dark, Grant set down his feast and picked up the videotape he had left on his chair.

"Watch two years after I've been gone," it read in

his wife's neat, floral handwriting. Ally had made a whole box of these tapes, "just in case." Most of them were for their daughters. Each tape was labeled with the child's name and the occasion for which she was to watch it. The next tape in the box was for Hannah's sixteenth birthday, which was four months away.

It was another two weeks until the anniversary of Ally's death, but Grant thought it would be okay if he watched a little early. It was their wedding anniversary today, and he thought he deserved it. He popped the tape into the VCR and turned on the TV.

Grant sat in his favorite chair, the one Ally had reupholstered for him in green-and-blue plaid for Father's Day three years ago. He hit Play on the remote and sat back to watch the TV in the darkness as he ate his mac and cheese and drank his wine.

The screen filled with light and Grant couldn't resist a bittersweet smile. He had come to terms with his wife's death, but seeing her like this still made him sad...and happy at the same time.

There she was, his Ally, sitting right here in this very chair. Her knees were drawn up and she was barefoot, wearing shorts and a tee. She wore a ball cap to cover her baldness from the chemo, but she looked great. She didn't look like a woman who was dying of breast cancer that had metastasized throughout her body.

"Hi ya, Grant," she said smiling.

"Hi ya," he whispered setting the bowl of macaroni and cheese down. He couldn't resist smiling back.

"Well, I guess if you're watching this tape, I've been gone two years." She met his gaze, and he could almost feel her in the room. "Because I know you," she said wagging her finger at him. "And you would never cheat. You would never break the seal on this tape until you were supposed to."

"That's what you think," he said under his breath. "Two weeks early, so there." He felt a silly impulse to stick his tongue out at her.

"Anyway," she said, almost as if she was conversing with him, hearing him reply. "I hope you're doing okay. I hope the girls are happy, healthy."

"They're fine," he said softly, unable to take his gaze off her. She had been so beautiful, his Ally, with her blond hair, practical short pixie haircut and hazel eyes. After the cancer and the mastectomies, she had worried that he would no longer think she was beautiful, but that hadn't been true. He had loved her, loved her body, right until the moment she drew her last breath. Even now…

"The reason I made this tape is that I've been worrying about you, Grant," she continued. "I don't mean that I'm worried about whether or not you're taking care of the girls. I know how capable you are. You've got the laundry done." She began to count off on her fingers.

"Folded and placed in baskets labeled with each girl's name," he murmured.

"You've probably got homemade meals in the freezer, labeled and everything." Ally laughed.

He laughed, too. Ally knew him so well. Last night they had eaten spaghetti and meatballs. The sauce had come from the freezer in a disposable container with the date labeled in permanent marker.

"You've probably got the garage cleaned out, the rugs vacuumed. The girls' rooms are probably neater than a pin—even Hannah's—and I know what an accomplishment that is."

Grant slid up in his chair drawing closer to the TV, as if somehow he could be closer to Ally. He missed her so much.

"And I know you still drop off the dry cleaning every Monday and pick it up on Wednesday on the way home from Becka's violin practice."

"Thursday," he said. "Mrs. Jargo had to change the lesson to Thursdays because she has her hair done on Wednesdays now."

"And I know the girls' homework is done on time, birthday gifts for parties are bought and wrapped and ready to go on the right day. I even know you probably got Jenna to make Halloween costumes." Again, that warm smile, that smile that seemed to envelop him like one of her hugs. He felt a tightness in his chest. He missed her hugs.

"But..." she continued as she pointed at him, "that's not what I've been worried about. I've been worried that you aren't taking care of yourself. Sure, I know, you get your hair cut every three weeks, your teeth cleaned every six months and you always iron your shirts on Sunday nights while you have family movie night. But what about *you,* sweetie? You've got to be lonely.'' She paused. ''And I know you don't know what to do about it.''

Grant held his breath, wondering where she was going with this.

''So I have a plan,'' Ally said, perking up. ''And I know you'll go for it because I know how much you like plans. How much you need plans.''

Grant shifted in his chair. A plan? She had a plan for what?

''The reason I didn't tell you this before...when I was still here, was because I knew you wouldn't listen to me. You wouldn't be able to deal with it. But now time has passed, sweetie. I've been gone two years and it's time for you to move on with your life. You deserve to be happy.''

Grant didn't like the sound of this. A part of him wanted to hit Rewind on the remote and just watch the beginning of the tape again. But he couldn't help himself. He had to hear what Ally had to say now.

''I think it's time you start dating,'' she said looking him right in the eyes.

He jerked back in the chair.

She put up one hand. ''I know, I know. You can never love anyone like you loved me. You don't want anyone else. Don't need anyone else. Well, I've got news for you, Grant. We all need someone. And if the roles were reversed right now, if I was sitting in that plaid chair listening to you say these words, I might not like it.'' She paused. ''But I would know you were right.''

Grant just sat there, staring at the screen. Never in a million years had he expected this.

Ally wanted him to date other women? He couldn't believe she was saying these things, couldn't believe she would leave a tape to tell him this. But that was his Ally, all right. She was a planner just like him.

''Now,'' she continued. ''I know this is going to be hard. Hard for you, hard for the girls. But give it a chance.''

''Date?'' Grant mumbled. ''Who would I date? Who wants a man who lives on a principal's salary with three girls?''

''I know, I know,'' she said almost simultaneously with his thought. ''Who would date you, a teacher with three girls?''

''A principal,'' he told Ally proudly. ''I got the principal's job last year when George moved to Maine.''

''So...'' Ally said carefully. ''I've thought this out. I know you're going to sit around for weeks saying no one would date you. Saying you wouldn't know who to ask if you wanted to go on a date. I've got that planned out, too.''

She stretched out her thin legs, and leaned forward in the chair. ''Jenna,'' she said softly. ''I want you to date Jenna. And, Grant, I think you'll fall in love with her.'' This time it was Ally's smile that was bittersweet. ''I think you'll fall in love with her and marry her. I want you to marry her.''

Grant grabbed the remote control, certain he had not heard right. Jenna? Ally's best friend, Jenna? Ally wanted him to go out with Jenna? Had she really said *marry?*

He fumbled with the remote. Hit Pause, cursed under his breath because he never cursed aloud, and then finally found Rewind. He rewound the tape a little.

"Jenna," she said again. "I want you to date Jenna—"

He *had* heard correctly.

"...I think you'll fall in love with her and marry her. I want you to marry her."

Grant started to hit Rewind again when he heard the back door open. He glanced up at the clock on the built-in bookshelves beside the TV. It was eight o'clock. Almost bedtime for the girls.

He heard five-year-old Maddy's sweet little voice, and he clicked the VCR off, then the power to the TV.

"Dad? Dad you here?" came his eleven-year-old Becka's voice.

He could hear light switches clicking on. Light from the kitchen suddenly poured into the hallway, reaching the den.

Grant got to his feet, torn between what Ally had said on the tape and his daughter's voice. "Here. I'm in here." He gripped the molding around the doorway as he stepped into the hall.

"Daddy!" Maddy ran into his arms. "Jenna got me another roll of gauze. You know I need gauze to wraps legs and stuff."

Grant gave pigtailed Maddy a big hug. She smelled of chocolate syrup and baby shampoo. He still used it on her hair because it didn't sting her eyes. Maddy wanted to be a vet when she grew up and she was always caring for patients, animate and inanimate. Every stuffed animal in the house had yards of gauze, tape, even toilet paper, wrapped around arms, legs and heads. His oldest daughter, Hannah, said it freaked her out to go into Maddy and Becka's room at night and see all of the animal mummies.

"Hey, Dad, Jenna found me some knee socks to match my uniform," Becka said, dropping a department store bag on the kitchen table.

"Hey ya, Dad." Hannah walked into the kitchen through the back door.

Last in the door was Jenna. Grant had seen Jenna a thousand times, maybe a million. They had been friends since their freshman year of college. Jenna had introduced Ally to him at a football tailgate party. But suddenly he couldn't take his eyes off her.

Jenna was nothing like petite, blond Ally. Jenna was tall with long red hair that Ally had always said was strawberry blond. She wasn't heavy, but she wasn't thin either. Curvy, that was a good word. Jenna was curvy with hips and breasts. Ally had always had a very athletic build, even after bearing and breastfeeding three children.

Jenna's eyes were green. Green with brown speckles. Her face was freckled and her mouth was...well it was sensuous, full pink lips, a tongue that darted when she spoke fast. And it seemed that Jenna was always talking fast.

"Hi," she called from the doorway, carrying in more bags. "Sorry we didn't get in sooner, but Becka needed the socks, Maddy wanted the four-inch gauze, not the two-inch, so we had to go to three drugstores and—"

"It was my fault, Dad." Hannah walked past him, giving him a peck on the cheek as she went by. "I wanted that new Chili Peppers CD and Jenna ran me all over town looking for it." She stopped in the hallway. "I'm going up to finish my homework. 'Night, Dad. 'Night, Jenna, thanks."

Becka rummaged through the bags Jenna was laying on the table, grabbed two, heaved her backpack onto her shoulder again, and walked by him. "Homework's done, 'night, Dad. 'Night, Jenna. Thanks for the cool stuff." She waited in the kitchen doorway. "Come on, Maddy. It's jammy time if you want Daddy to read the next chapter of Harry Potter."

"Harry Potter," Maddy said, a bandaged moose tucked under her armpit. "I love Harry. I'm going to marry him."

"You can't marry him," Becka said leading her sister down the hall. "It's like Dad. You can't marry your father, and you can't marry a make-believe person in a make-believe book."

Grant lifted his gaze to look at Jenna as he realized they were the only two left in the room. She was opening the refrigerator. "I stopped and got milk because Hannah thought you were low." She slid the gallon of skim milk onto a shelf and closed the door. She was wearing a dark purple raincoat over a sweater, long, flowered skirt and boots. Her hair was pulled back in a long ponytail, but little wisps had escaped the rubber band to curl around her face. For some reason, those curly wisps suddenly fascinated him.

Jenna met Grant's gaze. "You okay?" she said softly.

He glanced at the floor feeling silly. "I'm okay."

"You sure, because I know..." She took a breath and then went on. "I know it's your anniversary. That was why I thought tonight might be a good night to get this shopping over with." She started for the door.

He walked toward the door to see her out, Ally's words tumbling in his head.

Date Jenna? Ally wanted him to date Jenna. She wanted him to marry her.

She opened the door. "Well, if you don't need anything else, I guess I'll see you tomorrow."

"No."

She looked at him.

He shook his head. "I mean, no, I don't need anything else. Yes, I'll see you tomorrow." He offered a sheepish smile, having no clue what he was thinking or why he felt such confusion.

"'Night," Jenna said.

"Good night," he called.

Grant locked the back door, flipped off the lights again, and went upstairs to tuck his two youngest girls into bed. He read the next chapter of the fourth book in the Harry Potter series and then kissed his girls good-night. As he passed Hannah's closed door, he called, "Good night."

"'Night, Dad."

Downstairs, Grant went to the dark den again. Light from the hallway illuminated the table beside his chair and the cold macaroni and cheese. He sat down and took a sip of the wine. He stared at the dark TV screen.

Ally wanted him to marry Jenna? The thought was ridiculous. Beyond ridiculous. It was preposterous.

And then he thought of what else she had said. About him, about the way he was living.

He *was* lonely. He hated to admit it, but Ally was right. He was lonely and he missed his wife in a million ways, but mostly he just missed her being here. He thought that his job and his daughters would be enough to make him happy or at least content, but they weren't. He'd known that for months now. Something was missing from his life. Someone.

Grant didn't know how long he'd sat in the dark staring at the TV when he heard footsteps on the staircase.

"Dad?" Hannah called.

"In here."

She stuck her head in the doorway. Hannah was pretty like her mother with silky blond hair she wore pulled back in a short ponytail and hazel eyes that sparkled when she laughed. "You sitting in the dark again?" she grumbled.

He didn't know what to say, so he said nothing.

"Thinking about Mom?" she said in a quieter tone. "I know. I was thinking about her today, too. It was your anniversary."

Grant was touched that she remembered. "I miss her," he said, realizing that he didn't feel the same sadness he had once felt when he talked about Ally. It seemed that what people said was true. Most of the pain and sadness had passed. Now there were just a lot of memories in his head that made him smile.

Hannah leaned in the doorway. "Me, too." She glanced up. "But you know, Dad, she's been gone two years. You think maybe it's time you stop sitting in the dark by yourself at night, pretending she's here."

He got up and walked into the hallway, through to the kitchen. She followed him. "I don't pretend she's here," he said. "I just like the quiet."

"Well, whatever."

She hung in the kitchen doorway, and he wondered what was with teens and doorways. Hannah could never just walk into a room; she always had to stand in the doorway, as if she feared she might have to make a quick escape. What would he do when Becka turned thirteen? Would his two daughters share doorways or would they have to have their own?

Grant reached into the refrigerator and pulled out the gallon of milk Jenna had brought. He'd have to remember to include this in the reimbursement for all of the other things she'd gotten for the girls tonight. She'd been doing these things since before Ally's death, when Ally had gotten too weak to take the children out. Once in a while, Jenna would just herd them all into her car and head for a mall, or a movie, or something. It was a nice break for him, and the girls loved her.

"So what I was saying, Dad..."

He poured himself a glass of milk, not sure he wanted to hear what Hannah had to say, but listening anyway. He knew parents who would give their eye-teeth for their teenaged daughters to voluntarily offer their opinions on anything. To be able to have conversations with them that didn't involve shouting or accusations. But something told him that the direction Hannah was headed with this conversation wasn't somewhere he was ready to go yet.

"I think you should think about dating."

Grant knew he must have stood frozen for a moment because the glass almost overflowed with milk. He caught himself and capped the gallon container. So that *was* where she was headed. "Date? Me?" He laughed.

"Yes, you. Why not?" She lifted one shoulder draped in a thick sweater. "I don't know, Dad, you're still cute in a geeky kind of way."

He put the milk back into the fridge with a smile. "Well, thank you."

She exhaled. "You know what I mean. In a dad way."

He grabbed his glass of milk and leaned against the counter. "Hannah. Look at me. I *am* a geeky kind of guy. I'm not rich. I'm the principal of a school, for heaven's sake, and I've got three daughters to raise.

Who in her right mind would want to go out with me?'' He lifted his glass to take a drink.

Again, she raised one shoulder in a half shrug. ''I don't know. How about Aunt Jenna?''

She said it just as he took a big swallow of milk. He choked, snorted and thought maybe he had inhaled some milk.

''Dad? You okay?''

He choked again and tried to suck in a lung full of air. ''Okay…I'm fine,'' he managed.

She laughed. ''Careful there. Milk consumption can be a dangerous thing.''

You're not kidding, he thought, grabbing a napkin out of the holder on the counter to wipe his mouth. He couldn't believe Hannah had suggested he date Jenna. Was this some kind of conspiracy between her and Ally? He knew it couldn't be and yet…

''Well, I'm headed for bed,'' Hannah said interrupting his thoughts. ''Geometry test tomorrow, first period.''

''You study?'' he called after her as she disappeared into the hall. He was a principal now, but he had been a teacher first. Once a teacher, always a teacher.

''Yes, Dad,'' she called. '''Night, Dad.''

'''Night, hon.''

Grant finished his milk, rinsed out the glass and placed it in the dishwasher. Then he poured some soap in and hit Wash as he did every night before he went to bed. He turned out the kitchen light, headed for bed, then veered into the study as he realized he had left Ally's tape in the VCR. He wouldn't want one of the kids to find it. He meant to retrieve the tape, but when he got into the den, he had to watch it again. And again. It ended shortly after the marrying Jenna part. Ally just said that she loved him and that she couldn't have picked a better person to love him and their girls than Jenna.

Grant always went to bed by eleven. He brushed his teeth, folded his clothes and put on a pair of boxers before climbing into bed. But for the first time in his life, he fell asleep in front of the TV.

He fell asleep thinking of Jenna.

Chapter Two

Lights flickered on upstairs in Becka and Maddy's bedroom in the front of the cape cod as Jenna backed her Honda out of Grant's driveway and onto the street. "'Night sweeties," she murmured. "Sleep tight and don't let the bedbugs bite." She chuckled. "Don't let the weird dad bite is more like it."

Jenna knew it was Grant's and Ally's wedding anniversary today. She knew they would have been married sixteen years if it hadn't been for Ally's death from breast cancer. That was why she had taken the girls with her after school and done the dinner out and shopping thing. To give Grant a chance to be alone. Cry a little if he wanted to. The man certainly had the right.

She had expected him to be out of sorts at the very least when she brought the girls home, but what she had not expected was for him to be acting so strangely. What was with him tonight? Why had he looked at her in such an odd way?

Jenna crossed Route One, the main road through the southern Delaware beach communities and headed for her small neighborhood on the ocean side. Her two-bedroom cottage, left to her by her grandmother, was only four blocks from the beach. Over the years, real estate agents had tried again and again to get her to sell, or at least turn the house into a rental during the summer months. Houses like hers brought in an incredible amount of money June through August, she was told. But Jenna wasn't interested in money. She was interested in having a comfortable home to live in and providing a safe, happy environment for her sister, Amy.

Jenna turned onto her own street. The sky had grown dark, but the streetlamps illuminated the sidewalks and the small, older homes that lined both sides of the street. Seashell Drive was one of the streets that consisted mostly of year-round residents. Here, everyone knew their neighbors and no one had to worry about late-night partying next door in the summer. It was a nice place to live.

Jenna pulled into her driveway and grabbed her soft leather backpack that served as a purse as well as her book bag. She had some work to do for the kindergarten class she taught. She, Ally and Grant had all started at the Starfish Academy as teachers, then Ally had gotten sick and had to give up her job. Last year, Grant had been named principal when their principal had taken a job elsewhere. Jenna loved her job. She loved the school. She loved her students. And having Maddy Monroe this year just made it all the better.

Jenna let herself into the house with her key and flipped on the living room lights. The cottage was small with just a living room that also served as the dining room, a small galley kitchen, two bedrooms, a bath and a laundry/mudroom. What made the house, though, was the back porch, which her grandfather had closed in with glass panels. Even in the middle of the winter, it was warm and cozy on the sunporch, and plants thrived there as if living in a greenhouse. Beyond the porch, in the backyard, was a well-groomed garden of flowering plants, stone paths and dribbling water fountains that was Jenna's pride and joy. Even now, in September, when the days were growing short, the garden was alive with late-flowering plants, fresh herbs and even a tiny patch of peas.

Jenna tossed her backpack onto the couch and went back out the front door. At the house next to hers, she tapped on the door and walked in, knowing she was expected. She could hear the TV going and the sound of a familiar newscaster's voice as he reported on unrest in the Middle East.

"Your turn," Jenna heard eighty-three-year-old Mrs. Cannon say. "One more roll."

"But I haf to go. Bedtime," Amy answered.

Jenna and Mrs. Cannon had no trouble understanding Jenna's twenty-six-year-old sister, but she knew there were others who did. Amy's speech was gruff and halting, but it just took a little patience to follow what she was saying. Amy, born with Down's syndrome, was mentally handicapped and had been Jenna's responsibility since their mother died just after Jenna received her teaching degree from the University of Delaware.

"Jenna?" Amy looked up, bright-eyed and happy to see her sister when she walked into the living room. Amy and Mrs. Cannon were playing Yahtzee on the coffee table in front of the couch. The TV was on in the background, the sound of guns going off, low but audible, but no one seemed to be paying attention to the news show.

"I won. I won," Amy said, awkwardly waving her score sheet at Jenna. "Look, Jenna, I won the game." She beamed at her partner. "Mrs. Cannon says I'm a good Yahtzee player."

The gray-haired woman began to clean up the game. "You're the best I've seen," she said, obviously genuinely pleased to have Amy there.

It was an arrangement that seemed a gift from God to Jenna. Mrs. Cannon no longer drove and spent most of her time home alone, so she loved having Amy for company. And Jenna was fortunate to have Mrs. Cannon here to keep an eye on Amy whenever she needed her.

"You ready to go home?" Jenna asked her sister. "It's almost nine and I have homework to do."

"And I haf to take a shower," Amy told Mrs. Cannon, rolling her eyes. "Work tomorrow."

Jenna smiled. Amy worked at the Starfish Academy, too, as an assistant custodian. Her sister loved the job and enjoyed getting up every morning to go to it. Hiring Amy had been a brilliant move on Grant's part. Before her job at the school, Amy had been working at a shop that employed many mentally handicapped adults, but Amy had been bored there and hadn't liked it.

At the Starfish Academy she could easily handle the work that mostly included sweeping floors, refilling paper products throughout the school and picking up the grounds. Not only did she like the fact that she was good at her job, but she loved the excitement of being there with the children. Everyone loved Amy at the Academy, and they made her feel as if she were a part of something. With no family left except a brother who lived in Oregon, Jenna and Amy's family included the children and staff of the school.

"Thanks for having her over," Jenna said, always careful not to imply that Amy needed to be taken care of. Amy had become very sensitive lately to her own independence.

"You know I love Amy's company." Mrs. Cannon slowly rose from the couch as Amy popped up off the floor. "Having her sweet face around keeps me young."

"We can let ourselves out," Jenna said, giving the elderly woman a peck on the cheek. "See you tomorrow."

"See you tomorrow," Amy said, giving Mrs. Cannon a sloppy kiss on her other cheek.

Mrs. Cannon smiled. "Good night, dearies. Lock the door behind you."

"We will." Jenna ushered Amy out the door, turned the lock, and pulled it soundly shut behind her.

Amy ran across the yard, leaping over a small azalea bush. "Cold out here."

Jenna followed Amy across the yard. "Not cold, but chilly. It's late September." She pointed to the oak and maple trees that lined the street. "You see, the leaves are beginning to fall. Autumn is coming."

"And we can cut pumpkins," Amy said happily, clapping her hands.

"That's right, and we'll go to the orchard and pick apples and make applesauce." She opened the door for Amy.

"And Halloween," Amy squealed.

"And Halloween."

"And we can get dressed up like ghosties and tell everyone 'Boo.'" Amy's eyes were wide with the same excitement that Becka and Maddy had when speaking of Halloween, but that was okay because it was Jenna's favorite holiday, too.

Jenna closed the front door behind them and clicked the dead bolt in place. "Go get your shower and hop into bed."

"Will you read?"

Jenna glanced at her wristwatch. "Amy, it's late."

"Please?" Amy clutched her hands together. "Please, Jenna please. I'll wash real quick."

"Okay, but a real shower, Amy, with soap and shampoo. I'm serious."

"All right." Amy stomped off toward the bathroom. "I'll be right back quick."

Jenna reached for her backpack to take it to the dining room table where she would cut out apples and stems and worms from paper for her students for tomorrow. "Then just a short book."

"Inside, Outside, Upside Down," Amy chanted as she danced down the hallway, her short bobbed haircut swinging.

"Not that book again," Jenna groaned. Amy loved the Berenstain Bears. "We read that one last night," she called after her sister who had slipped into the bathroom. But of course, Jenna would read it again. She would do anything for Amy.

While she waited for Amy to finish in the bathroom, Jenna went to the dark kitchen to put on the kettle to make a cup of tea. As she leaned against the counter, she saw in her mind's eye an image of Grant leaning against his counter tonight, looking at her. He'd had the oddest expression on his face, as if she were a stranger he had just met.

The teakettle whistled and Jenna shrugged as she turned to fill her teapot with boiling water. *Men.*

"Good morning, Catherine," Jenna said cheerfully as she walked into the main office of the Starfish Academy the next morning.

"'Morning, Miss Cartwright."

Jenna smiled as she passed Catherine's desk on her way to the copy machine. Here at the Academy, every-thing was very informal between the teachers and administrators. Everyone on the staff called everyone else by their first name, even their principal,

Grant. Everyone except Catherine Oberton who insisted on using the same titles the children used. She had been Grant's secretary for more than a year, had known him for almost four, and still called him Dr. Monroe.

Jenna had punched her personal identification number and hit Print to make fifteen copies for her students as Grant came in from a rear door that led to the teachers' workroom. There was a copier in there, too, but Katie McAllen was hogging it. She hogged it every morning.

"Good morning," Jenna said to Grant.

He halted and looked at her with a deer-in-the-headlights stare. It was so funny that Jenna almost laughed.

"Grant?" she said. "You okay?"

He ran his hand down his red tie. Grant always wore a red tie, but this one had tiny flowers on it. "Fine, great." He nearly tripped as he turned to pass her in the small room and the toe of his shoe caught on the corner of a box of paper. Jenna put out her hands to catch him—as if all one hundred and forty pounds of her was going to catch all one hundred and ninety pounds of six-foot-one Grant.

"Easy there," she laughed, releasing her grip on his arm.

Grant's face reddened. "Sorry. Excuse me." He turned again to pass her, and this time made it successfully through the gauntlet.

Jenna turned to watch him retreat. What was going on with him? He was always so in control. Grant

Monroe did not trip on boxes of paper. He never had a hair out of place. The man was a deity.

Grant walked into his glass-walled office, and Jenna turned back to the copier that was trying to eat her original. She punched Print again. She had to finish up and get to class. She could already see uniformed cherubs in blue and green kilts and white shirts with navy ties hurrying down the hall to make it to their rooms before the late bell rang.

Jenna walked through the main office and glanced at Grant. He was sitting at his desk, but his door was open. She walked behind Catherine's desk and stuck her head in Grant's office.

"You okay?"

He glanced up and his pen slid across the page, dissecting some school form that Jenna guessed did not need to be dissected with a black line. "Fine."

"The girls okay?" she said slowly, watching him.

"Fine. Great."

She didn't believe him, but she had to get to class and she didn't have time for twenty questions. "Okay then," she said suspiciously. "Let me know if you or the girls need something."

He had righted his pen and gone back to filling out the form, ignoring the black line that now cut the page into two nice triangles. "Sure thing," he said, not looking up.

Jenna thought it was odd that he didn't make eye contact with her. They had always been good friends, and after Ally died, they had seemed to grow closer. Grant wasn't the kind of guy to cry on a friend's shoulder or reveal his deepest, darkest fears, but he knew he could depend on her.

Jenna glanced over her shoulder as she exited the main office into the hallway, and caught him watching her....

As Jenna walked out of the front office, it was all Grant could do to keep himself from lowering his head to his desk and pounding his forehead on it. He couldn't believe he had tripped over that box in the copy room while gawking at Jenna. He couldn't believe he'd let her startle him like that. He balled up the form he had been filling out, tossed it into the waste can beside his desk and grabbed another from a file in the drawer to his left.

Grant hadn't slept well last night in the chair in the den. His entire night had been riddled by strange dreams—Ally and Jenna on the beach calling him. Ally sitting beside him in front of the bonfire he had built for them. An anniversary celebration. But, when he had turned to her to offer a glass of celebratory wine, it had been Jenna beside him. The dream had been so real that he could still feel her warmth at his side. He could still smell that slightly flowery-musky fragrance she wore that permeated everything around her, her car, her house and even her classroom.

The dream had made him feel badly. Not so much because Ally was gone, but because he was dreaming of another woman. Never in all of the years of marriage to Ally had he dreamed of being with another woman and it scared him. He and Jenna had done nothing in his dream, but there had been feelings between them. Desires.

His face growing warm, he jumped up from his desk. The late bell had just rung. It would be time to do the morning announcements in a minute, he thought, pushing aside thoughts of Jenna and the smell of her.

"The morning announcements," Catherine, his secretary said, appearing at his side out of nowhere.

Grant glanced at Catherine with her tight chignon and wire-frame glasses. She was wearing a slim, dark skirt that fell well below her knees and a white blouse that tied in a big bow beneath her chin. It looked like something his grandmother wore. Though Catherine was the age he was, she always seemed much older to him. She would have fit perfectly with Grandma Cora's generation, had it not been for her flirtatious manner.

"Thanks, Catherine. Have you got those attendance numbers I need?"

She batted her lashes. The gesture was so overt it was almost funny. Almost. "Putting them on your desk, Dr. Monroe." She used the title, as if he were a world-famous heart surgeon who had gone to medical school for a zillion years rather than a guy who had gone to a local university at night to get his doctorate in education administration, while balancing a teaching job, a family and a new baby in the household.

Grant read the morning announcements over the intercom as he always did, ending with a quote from someone famous. Sometimes the quotes were serious, sometimes they were funny. Sometimes they applied directly to the pursuit of knowledge, and sometimes they applied to life in general, but everyone seemed to appreciate them.

The announcements over, Grant left the front office and Catherine's adoring eyes to walk the halls as he did each morning. The remainder of the day was spent tending to his duties and thinking about what Ally had said about dating Jenna. Attending a parent-teacher conference and thinking about Jenna. Sitting at his desk pretending to be diligently at work, while thinking about Jenna.

It was three o'clock and the school day was almost over when he strode out of his office, having no real purpose whatsoever except to change the scenery. Maybe if he took a walk, he could get Jenna out of his mind. Get what Ally had said out of his head. All day he'd heard his dead wife's voice in the back of his head like a never-ending audiotape.

Date Jenna. I think you'll fall in love with her and marry her…fall in love and marry her.

The idea was utterly absurd, Grant knew that. The trouble was that at the end of the videotape, Ally had made him promise he would give it a try. She had asked him to promise her that he would at least try one date. When he'd heard Ally's words, he had had no intentions of making any promises, verbally or otherwise. But the second time he watched the tape after the girls went to bed, the promise had just popped out of his mouth. Without thinking, he had said, "I promise."

So, a promise was a promise. Obviously, that's what the dreams were all about. That was why he couldn't stop thinking about Jenna. Because he had promised his wife. The logical answer to the problem was to ask Jenna out, have a nice evening and then go back to his den and tell his dead wife face-to-face that there was nothing between him and Jenna but friendship. No spark. Ally understood "the spark."

Grant found himself passing the nurse's office, passing the library headed straight for the kindergarten and first-grade wing. Headed straight for Jenna's classroom as if she were a magnet.

He rounded the corner, and nearly fell over Jenna, who was on her hands and knees on the floor of the hall, lining up wet paintings of what appeared to be apples...or maybe roundish fire engines.

Grant made a noise in his throat, caught off guard. He had almost stepped on her.

"Whoa," she cried, glancing up, smiling. Jenna was always smiling.

"What are you doing?" He slipped his hands into his pants pockets, not because he wanted them there, but because he couldn't think of anything else to do with them. Suddenly his arms were long, gangly appendages that seemed to serve no purpose but to make him look and feel awkward in Jenna's presence.

She began to crawl along the floor, spreading out the paintings along the wall. "We were doing watercolor painting this afternoon. Nice huh?"

He glanced over her shoulder. "Nice."

"Hey, I called about that software again, but I'm not getting anywhere. The guy said teachers can't place the orders, only 'the brass.'" She glanced up at him. "Think you're considered the brass?"

Today, she wore her golden-red hair in a ponytail the way his girls often did. It was the best hairdo he could manage when Ally had first gotten sick. He had branched out to pigtails, doggy ears and doorknobs, though ponytails were still his best 'do. But somehow the ponytail didn't look the same way on Jenna as it did on his girls. On Jenna, it was almost sexy.

He stuffed his hands deeper into his pockets. "I'll take care of it tomorrow. Leave the number in my mailbox."

"Great." She scooted along the floor, sliding more paintings against the wall, her fingertips tinted with wet red paint.

Inside the classroom, Grant could hear the children lining up to be dismissed. He could hear Jenna's assistant, Martha, giving last minute reminders. If Grant was going to get this over with, he was going to have to do it now. "Um..." he said.

She didn't seem to hear him. "Amy has soccer tonight. We didn't find those Cliffs Notes for Hannah, so if you want me to, I can track them down tonight. I have a few errands to run anyway."

"Hannah should not be using Cliffs Notes. She needs to read *The Crucible*. I read *The Crucible* in high school; you read it," he heard himself babble.

He stopped short, and took a deep breath. "Jenna, you want to go out to dinner Friday night?"

She glanced up at him, a soggy red paper in her hand with a name that resembled *Anthony* scrawled across it. She didn't hesitate. "Sure. That would be nice."

Jenna smiled and Grant relaxed. Hadn't been so bad after all.

"Great," he said. "Meet me at seven at that little French place you like?" He didn't have the nerve to pick her up. That would, after all, make it a real date, wouldn't it? "You know...separate cars in case I have to run home," he explained.

"Sure. Works for me."

The door to Jenna's classroom opened, and kindergartners spilled out. "Oops, better get to the buses," she said, getting to her feet.

Jenna went one way with her fifteen kindergartners, including his Maddy, and Grant went the other way. Only this time, his hands were in his pockets because he wanted them there, and he was whistling. He couldn't remember the last time he had whistled.

Chapter Three

"Daddy's got a date," Becka chanted from her perch on a stepping stool at the kitchen counter. She stirred the brownie mix rhythmically. "Daddy's got a date. Daddy's got a date," she sang.

"I do not have a date." Grant pulled the homemade chicken potpie out of the oven. He hadn't made the crust himself; it was refrigerator dough. But he still made a pretty mean chicken potpie, if he did say so himself.

"Daddy's got a date," Maddy repeated from the kitchen table. She was busy making a splint for a stuffed cat's tail. "What's a date, Becka?"

"I do not have a date," Grant repeated, pulling the corn muffins out of the oven.

"A date is when a man takes a woman to dinner or to a movie or something. Dad's going on a date with Aunt Jenna."

"I am having *dinner* with Aunt Jenna so we can talk in peace." Grant shut off the oven and slipped the flowered hot mitts off his hands. Jenna was meeting him at the restaurant, but if he didn't hurry, he was going to be late.

"Daddy's got a date with Aunt Jenna," Maddy sang, ministering to the stuffed tabby that rested on her dinner plate in front of her. "Daddy's got a date with Aunt Jenna."

"Be quiet both of you," Hannah said, coming into the kitchen. She was munching on a handful of celery sticks. "You're making Dad nervous. This is his first date."

"Does no one in this house hear me? This is not a date." Grant whipped off the red chef's apron he always wore in the kitchen to protect his clothing and hung it on its hook in the broom closet. All he had to do was grab his suit jacket off the dining chair and he'd be ready to go.

He had considered changing clothes after work, perhaps into a polo shirt and khakis. Something casual. But that would suggest this was a date, wouldn't it? And he didn't want to give Jenna the wrong idea. This wasn't really a date. It was just...he was just...fulfilling an obligation to his dead wife. That was all.

"Homework. Showers..." Grant began to tick off his mental list of reminders for Hannah who was baby-sitting tonight.

"No homework tonight, Dad," Becka said. "It's Friday."

"Okay. But only an hour of TV," Grant said looking at Hannah again. "No matter what these imps tell you." He gave Becka a squeeze as he walked behind her. "And no matter what they try to bribe you with."

Becka laughed and licked chocolate batter from her finger.

Grant leaned over Maddy to kiss the back of her head. "Bye, sweets. Be good for Hannah or I'll tie you up by your socks when I get home."

"Bye, Dada," Maddy said sweetly. "I hope you have a good date with Aunt Jenna. Don't kiss her too much."

Hannah burst into laughter. Becka giggled.

Grant looked wide-eyed at his two older daughters as if to ask, "Where did she get that from?"

His girls just shrugged.

Grant shook his head. He wouldn't ask, else he would certainly be late. He took a deep breath. His stomach was nervous and his forehead was slightly damp. This was a bad idea. Going out to dinner with Jenna was a bad idea and he knew it. He shouldn't be out with a woman. He belonged here with his children. But it was too late. He ducked into the dining room, grabbed his gray suit jacket and headed through the kitchen. He would just have to go through the motions of the dinner. Try to be good company and get out of there as soon as was reasonably possible.

"See you later, girls. Lock the door behind me. I have my cell phone if you need me," he said, checking to be sure it was on his belt.

"Have a good time. Be safe. No alcohol. No drugs.

Use your head. And call me if you need me to come get you, no questions asked,'' Hannah said, repeating the same thing Grant always told her before she went out the door. ''Love you!''

''Love you, girls.'' The words stuck in his dry throat as he went out through the laundry room into the garage. Inside his Explorer, he laid his jacket on the seat so that it wouldn't get wrinkled. Before he backed out of the garage, he took a tissue from the box between the two front seats and wiped his brow. As he wiped it, he caught a glimpse of himself in the rearview mirror.

Criminy, what was going on? Why was he so nervous? He looked petrified. He tucked the tissue into the garbage bag that hung behind the passenger seat and backed out of the garage and down the driveway.

It was just dinner with Jenna. Good old buddy Jenna. Jenna who he'd been friends with for a million years. Jenna who had been at his wedding. Been at the hospital for all his daughters' births. Jenna who had stuck by him when Ally had gotten sick.

He was nervous because it wasn't just dinner, no matter how he tried to convince himself otherwise. It was a date, and he hadn't been on a real date in twenty years. He was nervous because he was scared to death.

Jenna parked her car on the street and walked up the sidewalk to wait for Grant in front of the small French bistro just off Main Street. She was looking forward to dinner because the restaurant was so popular during the tourist months that no locals ever attempted to get in until the crowds thinned. She hadn't eaten here since spring and it was one of her favorite restaurants.

She spotted Grant's dark-blue SUV approaching up the street. She waved and checked her watch. Two minutes until seven. She smiled to herself. It wasn't like her to actually be on time, but it was just like Grant to be early.

She waited on the sidewalk for him to get out of his car, lock the door, then check to be sure it was locked—just as she knew he would. She pressed her hand to her stomach. She had butterflies.

Dinner with Grant was giving her butterflies?

She couldn't fathom why. She and Grant had shared hundreds of dinners together, before he and Ally had married, after the wedding, after Ally died.

But this dinner was different, and not just because he had asked her out to a restaurant rather than having her over to the house. It was something else. Something she couldn't quite put her finger on. Grant hadn't acted like himself this week. Ever since the evening of his anniversary, he'd been acting oddly and it was somehow related to her.

"Hi," he said, walking up the sidewalk, *GQ* handsome in his conservative gray suit, white shirt and red tie.

"Hi." She smiled. She had changed from her school "uniform" of a long flowered skirt and blouse into a dress. After she had changed her clothes, she had wondered if that was mistake. Would Grant think she thought this was a date? Women only change after work for dates. They didn't change for "just dinner with a friend." In the end, she had left the dress on simply because she liked the green-and-blue floral pattern and the way the fabric felt on her skin.

"How are you?" Grant said, sounding awkward. He leaned over her and she turned her cheek for the perfunctory hello kiss. It had been a tradition between them for years and yet suddenly it seemed different. She felt her cheeks grow warm as he kissed her.

He was wearing cologne. She liked the scent that was musky, but not overwhelming. He normally only put cologne on after he showered in the morning. What was the cologne for? Her?

"Do we have reservations?" she asked as he opened the door for her.

"For seven, on the porch."

She smiled. Of course they had reservations. Grant Monroe would never forget dinner reservations. Now *she* would forget reservations. She would show up fifteen minutes late because the cat got out. She would forget her purse. But not Grant. She had always admired his organizational skills. She had always told Ally that she could never live with the man, that he would drive her nuts, but she did admire him.

The hostess showed them to a table for two on the closed-in porch. There were fresh flowers on the linen-covered table and a candle. Grant pulled out Jenna's chair for her and then took his seat across from her.

Jenna accepted the menu from the hostess and smiled up at her. "Thanks."

"Your waitperson will be with you in a moment," the hostess said, backing away.

"So," Grant said, opening his menu.

"So," Jenna repeated. Then she peered at him from behind the menu like a kid pretending to be an adult. He was looking at her, too. She laughed. "This feels weird," she said.

He got a strange look on his face. "Bad weird? I didn't mean for you to feel uncomfortable. We could have gone somewhere else."

She laughed. Grant was nervous! She was amused, and oddly touched at the same time. And more than a little curious. Definitely curious. He had never been nervous around her before. What on earth was going on inside that organized head of his? What was he up to? Why had he asked her out to dinner? Jenna wanted to just ask him, but knew better. Grant, like most men, was not good at expressing his feelings. She knew him well enough to know she'd just have to be patient.

Jenna smiled and went back to looking at the menu. "So were the girls upset about you leaving?"

"Nah," he pshawed. "They were going to have my chicken potpie for dinner and then watch as much TV as they can squeeze in before they spot my headlights coming up the driveway."

"Mmm, I love your potpie, too. And *Goosebumps* is on the Nickelodeon channel tonight. I don't blame them for being tickled."

The waitress came to the table, introduced herself and poured water into their glasses. ''Would you care for a cocktail?''

Jenna glanced over the menu at Grant questioningly.

''Go ahead. You can have anything you want,'' he said.

She made a face. ''Of course I can have anything I want. I'm over twenty-one and I have the wrinkles to prove it. My question is, what are you having?''

''I don't know.'' He lifted one broad shoulder.

''Well, do you want a beer? Wine? Iced tea, what?''

He met her gaze hesitantly and lifted a dark brow. ''Maybe wine?''

''Wine it is.'' She looked to the waitress who waited patiently. ''We'll have the house Chardonnay.''

''Bottle or glass?'' the young woman asked.

''Just a glass.'' Jenna wrinkled her nose. ''First date,'' she said jokingly. ''I wouldn't want to lose my inhibitions and make a fool of myself, would I?''

The waitress laughed and walked away to get their wine.

Jenna glanced across the table to see Grant staring at her. ''I'm sorry. I didn't embarrass you, did I? I was just kidding.'' She couldn't read his thoughts for the life of her. ''About the date I mean.''

''It's all right,'' he said softly.

The look on his face told her it was.

''I like your wisecracks,'' he went on, surprising

her by actually offering his thoughts without her having to pry them out of him.

"How long have I been hearing you make those jokes?" He set aside his menu to look at her. Really look at her.

His total attention made Jenna feel strange to the tips of her toes. Warm. Comfy. Had Grant always been this attractive?

She grinned. "I don't know what on earth you're talking about. What jokes?"

"What about the time you introduced yourself as my second wife at that party?" he said, his dark eyes sparkling with the amusement. "*After* you introduced Ally as my first wife."

She laughed.

"At least I didn't say I was your girlfriend and the mother of your children."

He laughed with her, reaching for his water. He seemed to be less nervous now—actually enjoying her company.

"So how was school today?" Jenna picked up her menu again. She knew this wasn't a date, but it sure felt like one. It had been too long since she'd been alone with a man and it felt entirely too pleasant.

"Fine. The usual. Required forms to fill out. A meeting with some state guys. Arnold Smack was in for our daily chat."

Jenna smiled to herself. Any other principal would have expelled twelve-year-old Arnold ages ago, but not Grant. He seemed to have a soft spot for troublemakers. He was willing to give them a chance when no one else would.

"How was yours?" Grant scanned his menu.

"Oh, doesn't the baked brie sound wonderful?" Jenna pointed to the appetizer list. "My day? It was good. You know, the usual, though. We're on the letter *E.* We played eggplant football with a real eggplant. We had hardboiled eggs for a snack. We made elegant elephant ears to wear." She put her hands to each side of her head and flapped them like ears.

He smiled in a way that made her feel strange. A good strange. "What?" she asked. "Why are you looking at me like that?"

He shook his head. "Nothing. You," he amended. "I love how you get so excited about this stuff. You're so good with the students. Maddy loves you." He gestured, bringing his hand to his chest. "I mean Maddy already loved you, but now she loves you as her teacher, too."

Jenna didn't know what to say. She knew she was a good teacher, but having it come from Grant meant a great deal to her.

"Thanks. So what shall we have to eat?" she asked, looking back at the menu, afraid she might tear up. She didn't know what was going on with Grant, but she liked it. She liked the attention and she liked the way he was making her feel.

"I don't know. I was thinking scallops."

"Oh," Jenna breathed. "The scallops in the white wine and garlic sauce are so good here." She frowned. "But so is the grilled sea bass."

"Decisions, decisions," he teased.

The next hour and a half flew by and before Jenna knew it, Grant was walking her to her car. She had insisted she could reach her car on her own, that she was a big girl. She had parked under a streetlight and she had her pepper spray on her key chain, but he wouldn't take no for an answer.

She unlocked her Honda, yet hesitated to climb in. It had been such a nice evening. Jenna loved her sister dearly but she hadn't realized how much she craved real adult conversation. Ally had been her best friend since junior high. She had always had Ally to talk to and now that she was gone, there seemed to be this big void. Tonight, Grant had filled that void.

"Thanks for dinner," she said. It wasn't until that moment that she realized Grant had never brought up whatever it was that he had asked her out to talk to her about. She wrinkled her brow. "Grant?"

"Yeah?" He was standing beside the car. His car was in the opposite direction. He said he had to get home to the kids, but he seemed to be lingering.

"Was there..." She tried to figure out how she should say this. "Was there a reason why you wanted to have dinner tonight? I mean, did you need to talk about something?"

For a moment, it seemed she had startled him. He had that deer-in-the-headlights look again. "Not really. Nothing in particular. I just..." He let his sentence trail off into silence.

He hadn't wanted to talk about anything? He just wanted to have dinner with her? Did that mean this had been a *date* date? Jenna wondered. She didn't know what to think. A part of her was surprised. A part of her scared. A tiny part of her thrilled. It had never occurred to her that Grant might be interested in her in *that* way. Ally had been gone long enough that she wasn't surprised that he wanted to begin to date. It just had never occurred to her that he might want to date her.

"I just...just wanted to get out of the house. Speak to another adult without having milk spilt into my lap," he explained lamely. "That's all."

She was so surprised by the revelation that this might have been a real date that she didn't know what to say. "Oh, okay. That's fine." She slid into her car. "Well, thanks again. Tell the girls I said hi."

"Good night," he said, closing her door for her.

When she pulled away and glanced in her rearview mirror, he was still standing under the streetlights, hands in his pockets, watching her.

Odd. Very odd.

But a good odd.

Chapter Four

Grant let himself into the kitchen with his key and locked the door behind him. Humming to himself, he removed his suit jacket and slung it over his shoulder. "Hannah?" he called softly.

Becka and Maddy were already in bed, no doubt. He didn't want to wake them if they were asleep. As he walked to the staircase, he picked up a stuffed frog with one leg bandaged in toilet paper, a tennis ball and a box of crayons off the floor. "Hannah?"

She appeared at the top of the staircase dressed in a pair of sweatpants and her favorite old T-shirt that said U of D in faded letters. It had been her mother's. "Up here. Doing homework."

"On a Friday night?" Grant asked with surprise. He started up the steps, trying to keep his jacket on his shoulder while balancing the ball, the frog and the crayons. "Are you sick, babe?"

She wrinkled her nose. "Very funny. I have a paper due for English Lit in two weeks, and I thought I might get a head start on the note cards. Besides," she planted one hand on her hip, "it's not like I have anything else to do on a Friday night."

He reached the top of the landing. "Such as?"

"Such as a date." She threw her arms up. "I mean what kind of loser am I when even my dad can get a date and I can't?"

Grant cradled the toys in his arm and eased Maddy's bedroom door open. He slipped into the dark room that still smelled faintly of baby powder to him, though it had been years since it had been the nursery. He dropped the toys on a chest near the door and leaned over to kiss his youngest good-night. He backed out of the room and closed the door behind him.

"I told you, it wasn't a date. Jenna and I just had dinner."

Hannah eyed him slyly, then turned back into her room. "Okay, so how was your *non*-date?"

"It was…" As he followed his daughter, Grant tried to keep his mind clear, tried not to actually think about Jenna or the way she had made him feel tonight. "It was nice. The sea bass was excellent."

Hannah dropped into the chair in front of her desk and rested her fingers on the computer keyboard. "I didn't mean the food, Dad." She glanced over her shoulder. "You really are a geek, aren't you?"

He chuckled as he sat on the end of her rumpled bed. "I told you I was. Always have been."

She spun in her chair and leaned on its back. "So tell me the juicy details. I swear if I ever have my own date, I'll give you all the dirt."

He brushed at a speck of lint on the sleeve of his gray jacket lying beside him on the bed. "What's all of this talk about you and dating all of a sudden? I thought we had already agreed. No dating until you're sixteen."

"There was no agreeing to it. You just laid down the law. Besides..." She spun around in her chair to face the computer monitor again and clicked to another Web page. "No one is ever going to ask me out anyway. Not when I'm sixteen, not when I'm sixty."

"That's not true, Hannah. You're bright, you're fun and you make a mean western omelette."

She looked over her shoulder at him in disgust. "Dad, guys don't ask girls out on dates to make them breakfast."

"Well, I hope not."

She rolled her eyes and went back to the computer. "You know what I mean." She tapped the keys of the keyboard. "So you're not going to tell me anything about your date with Aunt Jenna? You're not even going to tell me if you kissed her good-night?"

Grant rose off the bed, taking his suit jacket with him. Suddenly his tie felt tight. Just thinking about kissing Jenna made him overly warm. He loosened his tie as he walked to the door. "Don't stay up too long."

"I won't."

"'Night, I love you, Hannah Banana."

"Good night, Dad. And stop calling me that."

Grant closed Hannah's door behind him and leaned against it for a moment. Kiss Jenna? Had his daughter lost her mind? What would make her think he had any intentions of kissing Jenna? It was just dinner out. A dinner to satisfy some foolish sense of honor he felt toward his dead wife.

Of course, he hadn't kissed Jenna. It would have been completely inappropriate.

So, why had he wanted so badly to do it?

The next afternoon, Jenna drove along the oak-lined street of Grant's neighborhood. She felt as if she was in junior high again. Following a boy down the Tech Ed hallway where she had no need to go, or circumnavigating the entire cafeteria, just so she could toss out her trash near some boy's table.

Jenna told herself she wasn't using Hannah's Cliffs Notes as an excuse to see Grant this afternoon. The teen really did want to read them. The fact that Jenna had gone to four bookstores looking for the Cliffs Notes on Arthur Miller's *The Crucible* merely showed her dedication to Hannah's studies.

She laughed aloud at herself. Who was she kidding? Hannah had said she was in no hurry. She said she could order them from a bookstore off the Internet. The only reason Jenna had tracked down the booklet today was so that she would have an excuse to drop by the house. To see Grant today. After their date last night, she just couldn't wait to see him in church tomorrow.

And it *had* been a date. She had told herself it wasn't, but it was. They had talked and laughed like a man and woman on a date. Like a man and woman *enjoying* a date. It was not her imagination. Something had changed between her and Grant and she liked it.

Just the thought of the quiet, intimate dinner they had shared last night sent tingles of excitement to the tips of her Nike sneakers. Absolutely nothing had happened between them last night. Not even a good-night kiss. But there had been an electricity between them, an excitement that Jenna had thought only existed in romance novels or old black-and-white movies.

Jenna had known Grant since college; she had introduced him and Ally. They had practically grown up together. They had graduated from college together; she had been in his wedding party. They had gotten jobs together at the same school. They had gone through the birth of his children and through Ally's sickness and death together. Grant and Jenna had been friends all these years, and she had never thought about him the way she was thinking about him now.

The truth was, she was attracted to him. Very attracted to him. And from the way he had acted last night, she thought he was attracted to her as well. The idea felt strange. Not unpleasant, just different. Ally had been dead two years now. Grant certainly had a right to date. Jenna knew Ally would want him to be happy.

But would Ally want Grant to be happy with *her?*

Jenna spotted Grant up ahead on the sidewalk, rake in hand. His back was to her as he dropped an armful of leaves into a wheelbarrow. He was dressed in a pair of worn khakis and an old navy polo. His hair was tousled from the wind.

And looking pretty delicious.

Jenna was half-tempted to ride right by. What would he think of her? Would he know this was all a ploy?

Instead of driving by, she signaled and pulled into the driveway. As she reached over to the passenger seat for the bag from the bookstore, she tried to calm her pounding heart. What was wrong with her? She had been here a million times before. There was no need for her to be getting all hot and bothered. It was Grant, for Pete's sake!

Jenna turned to open the door and started with surprise as the door pulled from her hand.

''Hey, there.''

It was Grant. Grant with a rake in his hand and a goofy smile on his face.

''Hey.'' She clutched the bag from the bookstore as if it was her shield of armor, and climbed out of the car.

''Fancy meeting you here.''

He was still smiling and she decided that the grin wasn't goofy at all. It was sweet—sweet and refreshing in an old-fashioned, goofy kind of way.

"I...the Cliffs Notes for Hannah." She raised the bag. "I just thought I would drop it off."

"You didn't have to do that." He held the rake in his hand and leaned on it as if he hadn't a care in the world. And he looked at her in a way that made her wish she wasn't in the jeans with the hole in the knee. She wondered if she'd eaten off all of her lipstick.

"I know," she stumbled. "I know she wants to get a head start on that paper."

He closed the car door behind her. Grant had always been a gentleman before, but suddenly it felt differently. More personal.

"Um...is she in the house?" Jenna looked up at him, into those clear blue eyes of his, and picked a leaf off his sleeve. "Hannah?"

"Hiding. They were all supposed to be out here helping me rake leaves," he explained. "Of course, they abandoned me one by one. Hannah got a phone call from a girlfriend. Becka had to use the bathroom, and I think Maddy was called into surgery. Elephant with a broken tail."

She laughed. "Not big on raking leaves, are they?" She walked beside him as he started for the house.

"So where's Amy?" he asked.

They walked up the driveway that was lined with carefully pruned azaleas. In the spring she knew they would bloom like burning bushes. "Bowling for Special People." She glanced at her watch. "I have to pick her up soon."

"That's right. Saturday afternoons. I forgot." Grant stopped on the stone walk that led to the front door of his white Victorian-style house. ''Hey, do you guys have plans for dinner? I mean if you do, that's fine.'' He studied the rake's handle. ''We're just having burgers on the grill, but...''

It was just burgers, but at this moment, Jenna thought she would have accepted a dinner invitation with Grant to have rattlesnake. She and Amy had eaten here a hundred times since Ally's death, but suddenly this seemed different. He seemed different.

''That would be nice. I have to pick up Amy, but then we can come back. You want us to grab some potato salad or something?''

He leaned on the rake, grinning. ''Potato salad would be good.''

For a moment, they just stood there looking at each other. Finally, Jenna forced herself up the walk. She waved the bag. ''I'll run this in to Hannah and then go for Amy. If Maddy wants to ride along, is that okay?''

''Sure.'' He gave a wave. ''See you in a little while.''

Jenna slipped into the house and closed the door behind her. She paused to catch her breath, thankful none of the girls were around to see her. She felt like a ninny. Like a girl with her first crush...and what a crush it was.

Though dinner had been over for an hour, the autumn air still smelled faintly of hamburgers and mesquite smoke. Jenna sat on the front porch swing beside Grant; the evening illuminated only by the lights on either side of the front door.

Grant gave a push with the toe of his Docksiders and the swing drifted backward. Through the open window to the living room, Jenna could hear the girls laughing as they played Clue. Becka and Maddy were playing partners and Hannah had kindly paired up with Amy. Judging from the sounds drifting through the window, they were enjoying themselves.

"Miss Scarlet did it in the library with—"

"Maddy, you have to wait your turn," Hannah interrupted. "And you already know it can't be Miss Scarlet. Becka, rein her in."

"Nice night," Grant said quietly to Jenna.

The girls' voices faded as Jenna leaned back on the white porch swing. They weren't sitting close enough together to be touching, but she could feel the heat of his body. She could smell the faint scent of soap and shampoo. He had showered while she was out picking up Amy and getting the potato salad.

Jenna loved the smell of a clean man. At least this one.

"Thanks for having us over," Jenna said, still feeling strange about the change in their relationship. Suddenly she was so much more aware of him. Aware of herself. What she said. What she did.

"You know the girls love having you here." He opened his mouth as if he intended to say something more, then let his words drift away on the breeze.

Across the street a car door slammed. A man strolled past the house and waved.

Grant and Jenna waved back.

"It sounds as if Hannah has a good start on her paper," Jenna said, wondering if Grant had wanted to say was that not just the girls loved having her here, but that he loved having her here, too.

"I know. Can you believe it? She's already started on it." He gave a little laugh. "Of course the way she explained it to me was that she had nothing else to do in her life."

Jenna turned to look at him. They drifted forward and then backward on the swing again. "What was that supposed to mean?"

"Boys." He rolled his eyes. "She wants to date."

"I thought there was a moratorium on dating in the household for those under sixteen?"

He laughed. "Well, she *will* be sixteen in a couple of months. And she has somehow convinced herself that no one will ever ask her out."

Jenna smiled. "Oh, I remember those days all too well. High school was not fun."

He sighed, sliding his arm along the top of the bench. They weren't sitting close enough together for his arm to be around her, but now his fingertips brushed the sleeve of her T-shirt as the swing swung forward and back again.

"I set that age requirement to give her a little time, but I didn't want her to think she *had* to start dating when she was sixteen. That's all she talks about—boys and how they don't like her."

"Grant, nearly every almost-sixteen-year-old feels that way. Don't worry."

He eyed her. ''I'm worried.''

''Don't be.'' She reached out and patted his knee. ''Hannah is a bright, responsible young lady. She'll be fine. She'll have more dates than she knows what to do with. What *you* know what to do with.''

''I know. I know.'' He paused. ''At least I hope I know that. I just want her to be happy. To like herself.''

Slowly Jenna pulled back her hand. ''Just give her time. She's got as steady a head on her shoulders as any fifteen-year-old I know. She's certainly more mature than I was at her age.''

The swing drifted back and forward again.

''Thanks,'' he said, touching her shoulder. ''I don't know what I would have done without you these last two years.''

Jenna didn't know what to say, so she said nothing. Instead, she gave the porch swing another push and enjoyed the feel of Grant's hand on her shoulder.

Chapter Five

Jenna leaned against the doorjamb as the copying machine hummed along making copies of marsupials for her class. Today they were working on the letter *M.* She watched the machine with one eye to be sure it didn't jam. With the other eye, she kept a close watch on Grant who was seated in his fishbowl-like office.

He was acting so strangely. It had been more than a week since their dinner date and the family barbecue that had followed the next night. Grant had seemed to genuinely enjoy her company. He seemed to be attracted to her, and yet, since that Saturday night at his house, he had definitely been avoiding her. When he made his daily rounds of the classrooms, he often missed hers. When she took all the girls out for ice cream the other night, he had bowed out, saying he had some paperwork to do for the Board of Education.

Jenna glanced through the doorway at Grant. His secretary, Miss Oberton, was perched on the corner of his desk, handing him pink slips of paper with phone messages. As she spoke, she swung one thin leg in front of him like a pendulum. She was obviously trying to catch his attention and Jenna was amused to see that Grant was clueless. Instead of noticing her leg, he nodded his head politely, accepted the messages and paid no attention whatsoever to her overt flirting.

The machine spit out the last copy with a great sigh, and Jenna had to abandon her post to grab her copies. Another teacher waited in line behind her. As Jenna retrieved the copies and her original, she wondered what she should do. Had she read Grant all wrong last weekend? Had it been her wishful thinking that he was attracted to her? Or was Grant truly enamored with her and just didn't know what to do about it?

Jenna knew it had to be hard for Grant, to start dating after all these years. She knew it had to be difficult for him to even think about another woman when he and Ally had been so happy together. But she also knew that he was lonely and that he needed someone.

Shoot. She certainly understood the kind of loneliness he must be feeling. When she thought back to the days when she and Paul had dated and then become engaged, she remembered how nice it had been to have someone to tell the boring details of the day to. She remembered how nice it was to have a man to share a bowl of popcorn and a rental movie with. Of course, the engagement hadn't worked out. Paul hadn't been able to accept Amy as part of the family they were going to create when they married, and that had been the end of that.

Jenna started down the hallway, her marsupials cradled in her arms. She knew that the best thing for her to do about Grant was do nothing. After all, so what if he did find her attractive? So, what if he was interested in dating her? To what end? Jenna had already accepted the fact that she would never marry. Never have a baby. Grant needed a wife, a mother for the girls, not a girlfriend with full responsibility of a mentally disabled sister. Jenna had already gone that route with Paul, and she knew it could never work. Men just couldn't, *wouldn't* accept the obligation she felt toward Amy, and it was unfair for her to expect them to.

Just let it go, Jenna thought as she passed a wall of poetry in the third-grade wing. He was probably avoiding her because he realized an attraction to her could go nowhere. Let him go. Keep things friendly the way they have always been, and hope for his sake that he finds someone.

Up ahead, she caught a glimpse of Grant as he rounded the corner. He must have escaped the clutches of the hungry Miss Oberton once more. Instead of turning to go down the kindergarten wing,

Jenna found herself following Grant. Her class wouldn't be back from music for ten more minutes.

Grant stopped at the water fountain to pick up a piece of paper off the floor. Without thinking, Jenna grabbed his arm. "Can I speak with you?" she asked quietly.

He looked up, clearly startled. There it was again, the old deer-in-the-headlights stare.

"Um. Sure." He glanced up and down the hall nervously.

She got his point. He knew this was personal and not about the soda machine stealing her two quarters again.

She tugged on his arm, dragging him behind her as she pushed through the men's room swinging door.

"J...Jenna... You can't come in here," he sputtered with alarm. "It's the men's room."

She had taken him completely off guard.

"What...what if someone comes in?" he stammered.

"What's the matter?" she asked as she released his arm, ignoring his protest. Her voice echoed off the pale blue bathroom tile.

"The matter?"

She sighed impatiently. Eight minutes and her class would be back. At this pace, it would take her all day to get through to him. "Why are you avoiding me? Did I say something last weekend to upset you? Did I do something to upset you?"

He looked at her, then at the floor, then back at her. "No, of course not. I've just been...busy." He gestured lamely. ''Hiring the new first-grade teacher, still working on placement testing with the sixth graders.''

He looked so cute, so caught off guard and out of his element, scrambling for excuses.

Jenna hugged her photocopies to her leaf-green sweater. She had absolutely no clue what she was doing in this men's room talking to Grant like this. ''Grant. I really had a good time that Friday night at dinner. The two of us…the hamburgers and the porch swing, too.''

''I did, too.''

He spoke as if he were thanking her for passing the bread.

''No.'' She met his gaze and touched the sleeve of his pressed gray suit jacket. She could smell his cologne very faintly, a designer fragrance from a department store that smelled far too masculine. ''I mean I *really* had a good time *with you* and…'' It was her turn to look at the bathroom floor tile.

What she wanted to say was that even though she had a good time, she thought it best they didn't go out alone again. What she wanted to say was that he didn't need to keep avoiding her. That she agreed it was best to leave their relationship the way it was.

''Jenna, would you like to go out again?'' Grant blurted out suddenly. ''Friday night? A movie maybe.''

Jenna lifted her gaze, fully intending to say no. Paul had broken her heart when he had refused to accept Amy. He had broken her heart when he had brought those pamphlets home to discuss placing Amy in a "facility." Jenna knew that dating Grant could lead to nothing but another broken heart. She had to be strong. She had to—

He met her gaze with those big, honest blues eyes of his, and she answered before she could think. Before she could stop herself from jumping off a cliff even though she knew she would hit the bottom hard. Even harder than with Paul.

"I...I'd love to go to the movies with you." Love to go to the moon, if you asked, she thought, feeling entirely too giddy for a woman pushing forty.

"Good. Great."

He smiled and she could no more have taken back her words than she could have taken back one of Amy's good-night hugs. "I'll call you?"

"Sure."

Grant was done. They had made their plans, but still she didn't move.

"Out," he finally said, pointing to the door. "Out of the men's room, Jenna, before we get caught." He pushed open the door, glancing into the hall. "I'll go after you," he whispered.

She slipped out and chuckled to herself all the way back to her classroom.

After work, Grant parked his car in his driveway because bicycles blocked the open garage. Maddy and Becka must have been riding after school.

Grant narrowly avoided an abandoned skateboard

and a scooter as he walked up the driveway, feeling slightly dazed.

He couldn't believe he had done it. He had asked Jenna out. After the night he had sat with her on the porch swing, he had known he had fulfilled Ally's request and need not make any further overtures. He hadn't intended doing it, but there it was.

Jenna had pulled him into the men's bathroom and the next thing he knew, the words tumbled out of his mouth.

If Jenna looked surprised, he knew he had to have looked doubly surprised.

And now that he had asked her out, now that they had agreed to go out Friday night on a real date, he didn't know if he wanted to jump over the azalea bushes along the drive, or bury himself beneath them.

A date. It was official. He was dating.

He was dating *Jenna.*

Maddy barreled out the front door and across the porch. "Dad! Tell Becka to give me back my snake."

Grant walked up the wooden steps that led to the front porch. "Real snake?"

Maddy wrinkled her nose the way her mother used to, and Grant had to laugh. Maddy barely remembered Ally any more.

"Fake snake, Dad. She took my Ka and said she wasn't giving him back." She crossed her arms over her chest and thrust out her lower lip.

Grant caught his pigtailed daughter's hand and led her through the front door. "And what, might I ask, did you do to Becka to bring on this retaliation?"

"Tell him," Becka shouted from the kitchen. "Tell him what you said on the bus."

Maddy slipped her hand from her father's and stared hard at the floor, arms crossed over her chest again.

Grant glanced down the hallway into the kitchen where he could see eleven-year-old Becka at the kitchen table doing homework. "What did you say on the bus?" he asked Maddy.

Maddy stared at the floor, her arms locked tightly. She was digging in, this bulldog of a daughter of his.

"She told Rowen McCarthy that I loved him," Becka shouted. "Gross! And it was right in front of everyone."

"You said you were going out," Maddy shouted down the hallway. "I heard you."

"Shut up," Becka hollered. "Dad make her shut up before I cut that snake in half with a pair of scissors." She held up the three-foot-long stuffed snake that already had an eye patch and pretended to cut it with her fingers.

"Daddy," Maddy shrieked. "Don't let her cut Ka up. He'll have to get stitches."

Grant grabbed Maddy's hand and led her down the hall to the kitchen. There was nothing like a little domestic disturbance to take a man's mind off a woman. "Maddy, apologize to Becka for what you said on the bus. That was not very nice."

"But, Daddy—"

"Apologize," he said sternly. He turned to Becka. "And you give her back her snake."

Maddy grimaced. ''Sorry,'' she shouted, sounding none-too-sorry.

Becka flung the stuffed snake at her little sister, who caught it and took off down the hall.

Grant walked into the kitchen and grabbed a glass from the cupboard, then filled it with water from the dispenser on the outside of the refrigerator. ''Where's Hannah?''

''On the phone. Where else?'' Becka spun in the chair and turned her attention back to her math book.

Grant downed half his drink, and then grabbed a pot from under the counter and filled it with water. He'd change his clothes before he started the spaghetti sauce.

Hannah strolled into the kitchen and returned the cordless phone to its base on the counter. ''Hey, Dad.''

''Hey. How was school?''

Hannah backed up to stand in her favorite place in the doorway. ''Fine. Missy got detention for not turning in her note cards again in lit class. We're supposed to order yearbooks next week.''

Grant leaned against the counter. He knew he needed to tell the girls he was going out this weekend. Needed to ask Hannah to baby-sit. And the sooner he got it over with, the better he would feel. He just wasn't sure how to approach the subject.

He reached for his water glass. ''Um...have any plans this weekend?''

She shrugged. ''No. Just the movie you're taking me and Missy and Jules to Friday night. Saturday I'll probably finish up my paper. I have a soccer scrimmage in the morning."

Hannah frowned. He must have reacted to her answer more than he realized.

"Why? What's up?"

He lowered his gaze to the floor. "Um...Friday night?"

"Dad. You promised you would take us to see the new Brad Pitt movie. Don't you remember? I told you weeks ago it was opening on Friday."

Grant turned on the burner beneath the pot of water. She was right. He had promised. He wanted to thump himself in the forehead for forgetting. A promise was a promise. He would have to call Jenna back and cancel.

The thing was, he didn't want to.

Grant groaned internally. What kind of father was he to think such a thing? Of course he couldn't put his own personal life ahead of his children's. He had an obligation to them and to their mother.

This was why dating was a bad idea. He didn't have time to go out with Jenna or with anyone else. He was too busy. He had too many commitments.

Grant walked to the refrigerator and removed a Tupperware container marked "Spaghetti Sauce 9/1" and slid it onto the counter. "Throw the sauce in a pot, will you, Hannah?" he asked as he reached for the phone. "I just have to make a quick call."

Hannah let him pass through the doorway, watching him suspiciously.

Grant slipped into the den and dialed Jenna's number. In a way, he was relieved. He wanted to go out with Jenna again. He liked her, but truthfully, she scared him. All these feelings he suddenly had scared him.

The phone rang in his ear.

"Hello. Cartwright residence," Amy said in her usual cheerful voice.

"Hi, Amy, it's Grant."

"Jenna and me, we're making paper bats," she told him.

"You are?"

"For Jenna's class," Amy said. "They are going to fly on strings, and Jenna says I can help tie them up."

"Wow. That's neat, Amy. Is Jenna there?"

"You want to talk to her?"

"Sure. Thanks."

Grant heard the phone drop with a bang, then Amy's voice in the background.

Jenna picked up. "Hey, you."

Grant turned his back to the den door so his voice wouldn't travel into the kitchen. He had talked to Jenna a million times on the phone and never felt this way before. Like he wanted her all to himself. "Hey, listen, about Friday night."

"A movie would be fun." She hesitated. "But another quiet dinner might be fun, too."

Oh, man, he thought. Now he really didn't want to break this date. She was practically coming out and saying she wanted to be alone with him. "Listen, Jenna. I...I can't. I promised Hannah I would take her and her girlfriends to the movies.'' He ran his hand over his head. ''And I just completely forgot.''

''So what you're saying is that you're ditching me for a carload of fifteen-year-olds.''

He smiled. ''Yeah.''

''Not just ditching me?'' she clarified.

He lowered his vice until he was practically whispering. He could hear Maddy and Becka talking in the kitchen but he couldn't be sure where Hannah was. He kept his back to the door. ''I'm really sorry. How about Saturday night?'' He grimaced. ''Shoot, no, Saturday won't work. I've got a finance meeting. We're trying to get that playground built in the park and Saturday night was the only night the other guys could meet.''

''Okay, so if Saturday won't work, why don't we just go together Friday night? What were you going to do with Maddy and Becka?''

''Maddy is spending the night with a friend. Becka was just tagging along with me. The movie is an action flick. PG rated.''

''So why don't I take Amy and Becka in my car?'' Jenna said. ''You drive the teens and we'll all rendezvous at the concession stand?''

Grant cradled the phone in his hand. ''You'd do that?''

She was quiet for a moment on the other end. Quiet long enough that he was afraid she was going to change her mind. ''I'd like to see you Friday night,'' she said softly in a way that made his palms sweaty.

"I'll take you how I can get you, busy father of three."

For a moment, he felt as if his ears were buzzing. Jenna's voice was so low and sexy on the phone. Why hadn't he ever realized that before? "Friday night, then. I'll get the details to you before then. Okay?"

"Okay," she said warmly.

"Got to go make spaghetti now," he said, feeling a little lost now that business had been taken care of.

"Talk to you later, Grant."

When she hung up, he just stood there for a minute, phone in hand.

"Dad's got another day-ate," Hannah sang from behind.

Grant spun around, startled. Had she been listening in all along? He felt his cheeks grow warm.

"Hannah! Are you listening in on a private phone conversation?"

Unashamed of herself, she sauntered into the den and perched on the edge of his plaid chair. "That was Aunt Jenna, wasn't it? And you're taking her to the Brad Pitt movie." She was grinning ear to ear.

"I'm taking you and your friends to the movie. Jenna and Amy are just tagging along."

"I knew it." She smacked her leg with delight. "I knew you and Jenna would get along."

"Of course we get along. We've been friends for years."

"Not that kind of friends," Hannah sang.

Now Grant was definitely embarrassed. He didn't know if he could deal with a teenager and a second round of his own teenage insecurities at the same time.

Grant's first thought was to deny what Hannah was insinuating right here and now. But, he had vowed from Hannah's birth that he would always be honest with his children, and he couldn't alter that vow now just because it made him uncomfortable.

"Do you mind? I mean is this okay with you?"

Hannah got up. "Dad, calm down. We're talking about a movie with Amy and Becka sitting between the two of you. We're not talking about hot sex."

This time Grant was sure his face turned red.

Hannah walked out the door. "It's okay, Dad. I'm happy for you. Spaghetti is on," she said as she disappeared down the hall. "I'm throwing in the pasta, so if you're going to change before dinner, do it now."

After Hannah left the room, Grant stood there in the den, the phone still in his hand. Suddenly, there seemed to be so much change in his life. Hannah was acting so maturely.

This thing with him and Jenna—he didn't handle change well. It was hard for him. Jenna sure as heck had thrown him off balance.

He thought of Jenna's sexy voice on the phone and smiled to himself as he headed out of the den. But maybe...just maybe being off balance was good for a man once in a while.

Chapter Six

"That was such a good movie," Hannah said, linking her arm through her friend Missy's.

"That man is *fine,*" said fifteen-year-old Jules, running to catch up with the other two girls.

"Whoa." Grant lifted his arms in the air as the three teens barreled past him and Jenna, and headed down the sidewalk toward the parking lot.

Becka linked her arm through Amy's. Amy giggled with delight and the two hurried after Hannah and her friends, leaving Jenna and Grant to walk to the car at an adult pace.

"So what did you think?" Grant asked.

Jenna lifted one shoulder. She'd had a wonderful time tonight. Just being with Grant made her feel good inside. The thought scared her and thrilled her at the same time. She knew nothing could come of this and yet, she couldn't help herself. She felt as if she was in a barrel tumbling over a waterfall.

"It was Brad Pitt," she said lightly. "How can a woman not enjoy a Brad Pitt movie? After all, that man is *fine,*" she said imitating the teenager.

He laughed. "He's your kind of guy?" Grant teased.

They had passed the movie theater's long row of glass doors and now walked along the sidewalk in front of closed shops. The parking lot was well lit, but beneath the shopping center awning, it was pleasantly dim.

She grinned. "Nah, not really. I prefer a man who is a little more...subtle about his masculinity."

"So your kind of man doesn't have to leap from burning cars, tunnel under mountains or drive motorcycles off cliffs?"

She smiled, enjoying the easy banter between them that was very close to flirting. It had been a long time since Jenna had flirted with someone. "No. My kind of hero can make dinner, sweep the floor *and* help children do homework, all at the same time," she said.

They continued to walk along the sidewalk. The theater had been busy, and they'd had to park on the side of the strip mall. The girls had all disappeared around the corner.

"Well then, hey." He lifted his hands, palms up. "I can do all of that and then some."

"I know you can." She glanced at him, suddenly feeling shy.

Grant sighed audibly and Jenna was afraid she had gone too far. "I'm sorry," she said quickly. "I didn't mean to—"

"You didn't mean to what?" he asked quietly.

To her surprise, he caught her hand and held it as they walked. They were taking their time now, enjoying the few moments they had alone together.

"You're sorry you said the nicest thing anyone has said to me in a very long time?" he questioned.

"No. I meant what I said. It's just that..." It was her turn to sigh aloud. "Oh, I'm not very good at this, Grant. I'm too old to be dating. I don't know what to say. What to..." Jenna let her sentence go without finishing it. "You know what I mean."

Grant halted on the sidewalk and turned to face her. There were cars turning on their headlights in the parking lot. Engines started, and doors slammed, but suddenly Jenna felt as if they were completely alone. It was if just the two of them stood in the darkness beneath the pet store awning with only the puppies to see them.

"I know what you mean," he said, holding her hand tightly.

He looked into her eyes as if he wanted to kiss her.

And Jenna wanted so badly for him to kiss her. Of course, what would she do if he did? It had been so long since a man kissed her that she probably couldn't remember how to do it.

Jenna was tempted to just turn away, to run for the car. She could hear Hannah talking with her girlfriends around the corner. She could hear Amy giggling.

"Grant—"

"Jenna," he said his voice surprisingly shaky. "I want to kiss you so badly. I just..." He gazed downward.

"You just what?" she whispered. He couldn't? Couldn't because of Ally?

"I just..." Slowly he dragged his gaze upward until he met hers again. He gave a nervous laugh. "What if I don't know how to kiss anymore? It's...it's been a long time since I've felt a woman's lips on mine."

His words melted Jenna's heart. He looked so sweet. So scared. She was going to tell him it was all right. Tell him she was thinking the same thing. Instead, she lifted on her toes and slid her hands upward over his chest. Very slowly, taking her time, never breaking eye contact, she raised her mouth to his.

Grant's lips met hers, his touch hesitant, as if he still wasn't sure he really wanted to kiss her.

But the smell of his cologne, his clean hair and his body overwhelmed her just the same. The heat of his body drew her closer. She slid her arms around his neck and felt his hands tighten at her waist.

She parted her lips slightly and their breath mingled. She felt light-headed and unsteady on her feet. Had it really been four years since she had felt a man's mouth on hers?

"I've wanted to do this so badly," he breathed.

To her surprise, instead of releasing her, Grant

tightened his hold around her waist. He lifted the other hand to caress her cheek and his mouth pressed hard against hers.

Her lips parted of their own accord and she tasted the tip of his tongue. Jenna was glad he was holding her, because at that moment she knew she swayed on her feet.

Grant was the best thing she had ever tasted in her life. He definitely won over champagne and raspberries, hands down.

As their tongues met and tasted one another, she felt as if the earth suddenly tilted on its axis. She was completely overwhelmed by the taste of him, the scent of him, the feel of his arms around her.

They finally parted, breathless and panting, nothing seeming the same as it had been a moment before.

Jenna brought her fingertips to her lips. "Wow," she murmured.

"Wow," he repeated.

She lifted her gaze to meet his and met with his smile. "Wow-ee," she repeated again foolishly.

"Dad!" Becka darted around the corner. "Hannah says I'm a worm. She called me a worm in front of her friends and embarrassed me."

Grant took a step back from Jenna. He seemed unsteady on his feet, too.

Becka apparently didn't notice how closely they had been standing together.

Grant dropped one arm over his daughter's shoulder. Jenna was amazed by how quickly he could shift gears.

"Come on, worm of my heart." He started for the car again, leading Becka. "You can sit in the front on the way home."

"Dad. I can't believe *you're* saying it now. You're really not very funny, you know."

"Coming, Jenna?" Grant didn't turn to her, but he opened his free hand and reached back to her.

Jenna hurried to catch up and grabbed his hand. She could still taste his mouth on hers. She was flustered, wobbly, dying for another kiss....

Who would ever have thought calm, well-organized, predictable Mr. Gray Suit and Red Tie could kiss like that?

The following evening, Jenna sat in her car, parked in front of the bowling alley waiting for Amy. At first, the church-sponsored Bowling for Special People had been held only one night a month. But it had been such an overwhelming success that it had been expanded to every Saturday afternoon. Unfortunately, the bowling alley had been booked all this Saturday afternoon for a special event, so Amy had not been able to meet her friends until evening. Jenna checked her watch. It was one minute until nine. Amy would be out any time now.

Her cell phone rang, and she picked it up off the seat of her Honda. When she saw the name and number come up on the tiny phone screen, she smiled. It read Grant.

He had already called three times today. The first time was to thank her for the date the night before—

pretty legitimate. The next time was to ask her if it was okay to trim his boxwood in the backyard this late in the fall—a little lame. The last time he had called to ask her if he could substitute green pepper for red pepper in a stir-fry recipe—definitely lame, since he did more cooking than she did.

She answered the cell phone. "Hi."

"Hi." Grant's voice was so warm and sexy that she felt as if he was right here beside her in the dark car. "What are you doing?"

"Waiting for Amy. Remember, I told you, bowling was pushed back to evening tonight. Too many birthday parties or something."

"That's right." He chuckled. "Actually I did know you were there waiting for Amy. I called the house and then remembered where you said you would be."

"Did you leave a sexy message on my machine?" There was no way around it. She was definitely flirting with him now.

He chuckled, but his voice was still soft. "Thought about it. I actually called a second time," he confessed sheepishly. "I just couldn't think of a message to leave so I hung up."

She laughed. His sweet confession was even better than a message on her machine.

"I didn't call for anything this time," he continued. "Couldn't think of any more excuses to call so I just called."

"I'm glad you did." She smiled. "Why are you talking so quietly?" she asked shifting on the car seat.

She was glad Amy was running late tonight. Glad to have these few moments "alone" with Grant.

"Hiding."

"Hiding?"

"In the den. The girls are in the kitchen cleaning up the dishes from dinner. We played ball in the yard after we ate, so we're just getting to clean up."

"And you're hiding from them?"

"I get on Hannah about being on the phone so much," he said sheepishly. "Guess I didn't want to hear it from the girls." He paused. "I don't mean that because it's you," he went on quickly. "It's just that—"

She laughed. "You don't have to explain yourself, Grant. I understand. We have to remember, this is new for us, but it's new for the girls, too. I…I think we need to give them time to get used to seeing us together." Again, she wondered briefly to what end, but she pushed that thought aside before it had time to take root.

"Well, I guess I should go," Grant told her. "They're arguing over whose turn it is to sweep. I think it's Becka's, but she's putting up a good argument."

"Ok, I'll let you go." She paused. "Grant."

"Yeah?"

"I really am glad you called," she said quietly as if she, too, were hiding.

"Me, too. 'Night. See you in church in the morning."

"See you in church." Jenna hit the end-call button

and dropped the phone on the car seat. She glanced at her watch. It was six minutes after nine. Where was Amy?

Jenna glanced up. She saw several cars she recognized pulling out of the parking lot. Apparently Amy's group had finished and everyone was being picked up. So, where was Amy?

Jenna grabbed the keys and climbed out of the car. She walked up to the lit entrance, looking through the glass doors. Maybe Amy was waiting inside the lobby, though usually she walked out onto the curb. Or maybe she had gone to the bathroom. Jenna would find one of the volunteers if she didn't find Amy.

As Jenna reached for the door handle, she saw a young man in a lip lock with a woman. She could only see the back of the man's head and jean jacket because he had the woman backed against the wall. She frowned. How inappropriate for a public place.

Then her cheeks grew warm. How was this any worse than what she and Grant had done on the sidewalk last night?

Jenna stepped into the lobby. As she passed the man and woman now embracing, she caught sight of something out of the corner of her eye. A bright-pink sweatshirt sleeve.

Amy had worn her hot-pink sweatsuit tonight. Amy wore only sweatsuits because they fit her stocky body and because they were easy for her to manage alone. The hot-pink suit was her favorite.

Jenna turned to get a second look. Her mouth dropped. "Amy Cartwright," she shouted.

Her voice startled the young man and woman. It startled her. She hadn't meant to shout.

The young man in the jean jacket backed up, lowering his gaze in obvious guilt.

"Jenna," Amy said, not seeming to realize she should have been embarrassed. "I didn't know you were here."

"Didn't know I was here? Amy, I've been waiting in the parking lot for you like I do every Saturday. I was worried when you didn't come out so I came looking for you."

Jenna focused on the young man. This had caught her completely off guard. A man kissing Amy? How dare he take advantage of her sister. She'd call out the bowling alley manager. She'd call the cops.

"Who are you?" she demanded of the young man. "And what do you think you're doing to my sister?"

Amy broke into a big smile. "This is my friend Jeffery," she said, clasping her hands and swinging her body. "He just moved to the beach. He likes to bowl, too."

When Jenna took a step closer and Jeffery raised his head, she realized that he, like Amy, had Down's syndrome.

Jenna had done so much studying as a teen about her sister's diagnosis that she recognized the features immediately. Jeffery was obviously a part of Amy's church group.

Jenna took a step back, even more caught off guard now. "Jeffery...do you have a ride home?"

He nodded rapidly. "My brother, he picks me up

and takes me to Logan House. That's where I live now.'' He looked at Amy. ''A blue truck. We have a blue truck. Ford F150 pickup. V8 engine. Bed liner.''

Amy grinned. ''Jeffery likes cars. He knows a lot about cars.''

''And trucks,'' he told Jenna, beaming. ''I know a lot about trucks.''

Jenna held out her hand to Amy. ''Let's go,'' she said sharply.

Amy caught her sister's hand and shuffled after her. ''See you on Saturday, Jeffery.'' She gave a jerky wave.

''See you Saturday. Maybe my brother will let me show you the F150 pickup.''

Jenna pulled hard on Amy's arm. ''Come on. It's late.''

At the car, Amy shuffled around the front and climbed into the passenger side. She hooked her seat belt.

Flustered, Jenna fumbled with the key. She couldn't get the darned thing in the ignition.

In the past, she had certainly had to deal with difficult issues with Amy—when their mother had died, when Amy had started her period, when she wanted a new job that was more challenging.

But never had Jenna considered that a boy—no, Jeffery was not a boy; he was a man. Twenty-five at least. Maybe older. She had never considered that a man might be attracted to Amy.

Jenna threw the car into reverse and backed out of the parking space. She hit the brakes a little harder than she had intended, then pushed the shift into drive and pulled out of the lot. She turned onto the street.

"You're mad at me," Amy said, two blocks from the bowling alley.

"I'm not mad at you." Jenna felt silly the minute the words came out of her mouth. Amy was right. She was angry. Angry and afraid. Amy knew nothing of what went on between a man and a woman. She wasn't capable of that kind of relationship. Jeffery was taking advantage of Amy and she wouldn't have it.

Amy was silent for a minute. "Yes, you are," she said, a stubborn tone to her voice.

"Amy," Jenna said, forcing herself to speak calmly. "What were you doing with Jeffery in the lobby?"

"I kissed him good-night."

"He shouldn't have kissed you."

"I kissed *him* good-night," Amy repeated.

"Well...you shouldn't have."

"He's my friend," Amy defended.

"I understand that. But remember, we don't kiss all of our friends and those who we do, we only kiss them on the cheek, right?" She glanced sideways at Amy, then back at the road. The wind was blowing dry leaves and grass across the pavement.

Jenna had talked about kissing and hugging before with Amy. One of the traits of Down's syndrome people was that they were very affectionate. Jenna had had to work with Amy about how to be affectionate with others without being inappropriate, or making them uncomfortable. Amy knew the rules, and though she was still very touchy with people, she stayed within the right boundaries. Until tonight.

When Amy didn't answer, Jenna let the subject drop. They drove home in silence. The minute she parked the car, Amy jumped out and ran to the door. She stepped back to let Jenna use the key.

Inside the dark living room, Amy stomped across the floor, headed for her room. "I was just kissing Jeffery good-night," she shouted. "And I'll kiss him if I want and you can't tell me not to!" She walked into her bedroom and slammed the door shut.

Jenna just stood in the darkness for a moment. She didn't know what to do. Amy had never hollered at her like this before. Never slammed her bedroom door.

Feeling a little shaky, Jenna locked the front door. She walked to the kitchen to put on tea, and then went to her own bedroom to change into her cozy flannel pj's. This pair had wildflowers all over them.

As she made herself a cup of tea, she considered going in to speak to Amy, but decided against it. The door was shut and the agreement between them had always been not to intrude beyond closed doors. Everyone had a right to some privacy.

Jenna took her cup of tea and the phone to the couch and curled up with her afghan. For a long time, she sipped her tea and stared at the phone. It was ten-thirty before she finally picked it up.

Thankfully, it was Grant who answered and not

Hannah. Had it been Hannah, Jenna might have been tempted to hang up.

"Grant?" she said. "It's me, Jenna."

She must have come across badly, because his voice was filled with concern. "Jenna, what's wrong?"

She brushed at her damp eyes, felling silly. It had been a silly argument. She knew she could talk to Amy tomorrow and everything would be fine. Just hearing Grant's voice made her feel better.

"I had an argument with Amy tonight. Not about taking a shower, or changing her socks every day." She took a breath. "Grant, I caught a man kissing Amy tonight at the bowling alley."

When he didn't immediately respond, she repeated herself. "Did you hear me? A man was kissing my sister!"

"Do you think he was taking advantage of her?" he said, obviously choosing his words carefully.

"Of course he was taking advantage of her," she blurted. "Amy doesn't understand what that kind of kissing is. She doesn't understand where it can lead."

"Jenna, it's going to be okay, just calm down."

"I am calm!" She took a deep breath, realizing she had raised her voice. "I'm not calm, am I?"

She could almost hear his smile.

"No, you're not."

Jenna was surprised that she was close to tears. She took another deep breath. "Grant, I don't think he was taking advantage of her. She was grinning ear-to-ear when I broke it up. She told me it was her idea to kiss him goodbye."

"I see." He paused. "You know, Jenna, she *is* a young woman. How many guys had you kissed by the time you were twenty-six?"

"It's not the same thing, and you know it."

He didn't answer right away, his lack of a reply expressing more than words could have.

"You understand why I'm worried," she said in frustration. "You know Amy. You know what she is and isn't capable of understanding."

"I certainly think you have a right to be concerned. To keep an eye on her, but honestly, Jenna, a kiss in the bowling alley parking lot won't hurt her. She has a right to live. A right to be a part of this world and all of the things it entails, just like you and me. You, of all people, know that."

Jenna reached for her cup of tea, calmer now. "You're right," she sighed. "Of course you're right. I just don't want her to get hurt. I don't want anyone to take advantage of her."

"Of course you don't," he said gently. "So you talk to her, and maybe to the young man. I'm assuming he's part of her bowling group."

"He is. He has Down's, too." Jenna groaned and ran one hand over her head as she drew her legs up onto the couch. "You know, this never occurred to me. I never thought this problem would ever come up with Amy."

He chuckled. "You've encouraged her to be independent. The job at the school, taking care of her own needs at home. It's only natural that she would make her own friends."

"Friends, I understand, but a boyfriend?" Jenna whispered.

Again, he chuckled. "It's going to be all right," he assured her in his low, sexy voice.

Jenna bit down on her lower lip. The room was dark and talking to Grant on the phone like this made her feel as if he was in the room with her...almost. She wished he was here with her now, holding her in comfort. The episode between Amy and Jeffery had rattled her on more than one level. Her sister was growing up in some ways that Jenna could not control. How would she cope? What would Amy do next? "You think so?"

"I know so."

She smiled. "Thanks."

"You're welcome."

A pause stretched between them. Neither seemed to want to hang up even though the conversation was obviously over.

"Well," Jenna finally said. "I should let you go. It's late."

"I'll talk to you tomorrow," he said. "And Jenna..."

"Yeah?"

"I'm glad you called me," he murmured. "Glad you thought you could call me about this." His words weren't as good as a good-night kiss would have been, but they were close.

Chapter Seven

Grant pulled up in front of Jenna's house and parked the car along the street. "Be right back," he called over his shoulder.

Becka didn't look up from the Gameboy on her lap. Maddy lifted a stuffed gorilla's arm that was wrapped in gauze and waved for the pet. "Hurry up, Dad, before someone else gets all of the good pumpkins."

"There are plenty of pumpkins, Maddy." He climbed out of the car. "A whole field of pumpkins to chose from." He covered the distance to Jenna's door, knocked and entered. She was expecting him.

"Grant, that you?" Jenna called as she stuck her head out the bathroom door. It was wrapped turban-style in a towel. "I'll be just another minute. Amy!" she called down the hall. "Grant's here. Let's go pick some pumpkins."

Grant checked his watch. Noon. He'd told Jenna

he would be here by noon, but of course she wasn't ready. She was rarely ready on time. Well, at least she was dressed.

He exhaled. Her lack of punctuality made him crazy. He glanced around the small living room. Piles of schoolwork littered the floor, end tables and coffee table. A pair of sneakers and a sweatshirt lay on the floor in front of the couch. Not one, but two, tea mugs were on the coffee table. Half a lacy lavender bra poked out from beneath the couch.

He averted his eyes. Jenna's untidiness made him crazy, too.

He grabbed the two teacups and carried them to the kitchen sink that was full of dirty dishes.

They had been dating—seriously dating—for a month now, and he was torn. He really liked Jenna, and the girls seemed to be pleased he was seeing her. She was so thoughtful, so sweet, funny, fun. And she was a mess. He had never realized before just how unorganized she was.

He heard the blow-dryer come on in the bathroom.

"Hi, Grant!" Amy bounded into the living room and through the front door. "I'll wait in the car."

Grant returned to the living room. He had been happy this last month. Jenna seemed to fill an ache in his life, an ache he hadn't even realized was there until their first date. But now, he was beginning to wonder just where this was leading.

He thought about Ally and the videotape. She wanted him to marry Jenna.

Marry Jenna? He grabbed the nearest stack of

newspapers and carried them to the laundry room and tossed them in the recycling bin. How could he marry a woman who could actually leave a house with a sink full of dirty dishes?

He returned to the living room and scooped up the sweatshirt. He'd toss it in the laundry room where he knew there would be piles of dirty clothes on the floor. How could he ever marry Jenna and live with piles of dirty laundry?

But then he thought about her kisses. They were few and far between, most stolen in his hallways, or in the driveway after a date that included one or more children. But her kisses made him feel so alive. Her touch, the sound of her sexy voice in his ear, made him feel as if he had more purpose in life than caring for his children and pushing papers as the principal of a school. She made him feel as if he was a part of the world. As if he fit in. She made him feel loved in a way his kids could not.

Shocked that the l-word had come to mind, he grabbed Jenna's bra off the floor. He'd throw it and the sweatshirt into the laundry room.

"Can I help you?"

Grant straightened, the lavender bra dangling from one hand; a C-cup for sure. The black sweatshirt with bats on it hung from his other hand.

Jenna glanced at her bra, a look of amusement on her face.

Grant felt his cheeks grow warm and then he felt silly for being embarrassed. He went to stores and bought bras for Hannah, for heaven's sake. He'd helped Becka buy her very first bra only last year.

But this was a whole other ball game. He glanced at the bra, then at Jenna. "I...I was just helping you straighten up a bit," he stammered and cleared his throat. "While you were getting ready."

Luckily, she burst into laughter. "Give me that." She snatched the bra from his hand, not in the least bit embarrassed. "And that, I'm wearing," She took the sweatshirt as well. She leaned toward him, puckering her lips.

He brushed his lips against hers and fought the impulse to close his eyes. To linger over her lips. The kids were waiting outside. Besides, the last couple of times they had kissed, it had gotten a little hot and heavy. He wasn't satisfied just to kiss her any more. He wanted to touch her, and not just her face, or her arms. When he kissed her, his hands ached to caress her breasts. He ached to caress her...

He swallowed hard and took a step back. "Um, Amy is already in the car. Ready to go?"

She tossed the bra over her shoulder and onto the couch. "Ready." She grinned.

He shook his head in exasperation. He knew he wasn't going to change her untidiness any more than she was going to change his compulsive need to be neat. If there was one thing he'd learned in almost forty years, it was that you had to accept people for who they were and not try to change them.

He followed her out the door, locking it behind them.

* * *

Becka, Amy and Maddy all leaped out of the car at Uncle Albert's Pun'kin Patch, and raced down the dirt path toward the three acres of vines. Coming to Uncle Albert's had been an autumn tradition of theirs since Hannah was old enough to dress in a black cat costume and go trick-or-treating.

Grant walked around to Jenna's side of the car as the girls ran down the road. ''You know, this is the first time I've ever been here without Hannah,'' he mused aloud.

Jenna grabbed his hand and they headed down the dirt road like a couple of old married folks out with the kids on a Saturday afternoon. ''With the boyfriend again?''

He nodded. ''She and Mark are *studying* at his house for a history test.''

She glanced sideways at him. ''You worried she's doing more than just studying?''

He lifted one shoulder. ''Actually, I've been trying not to think about it at all. Some boy kissing my daughter.'' He made a face.

Jenna laughed and patted Grant's arm. ''Let her have a little fun. This is her very first real boyfriend. This is an exiting time in her life.''

He raised his brows. ''She informed me last night they were 'going together.' What's that supposed to mean?'' he grumped. ''I asked her where they were going, but she didn't laugh.''

Jenna swung Grant's arm playfully. ''She'll be fine. She's not going to do anything she shouldn't. You've raised her too well for that. She respects herself too much for what you're thinking and you know it."

"I know. You're right. I know you're right. I'm just concerned it's too much too fast. A month ago she was moaning that no one would ever be interested in her. Now, even without any official dates, it seems as if she spends every waking moment with this pimple-faced boy. Every day they're doing something at school or going to his house to study. I just don't want her to get hurt, that's all."

"Dad! What do you think of this one?" Maddy called from a hundred feet away. She was making her stuffed gorilla dance on a pumpkin that was almost as big as she was.

"Too big to fit in the back of the car," he called. "Find another one. A *smaller* one."

Maddy laughed and bounced off in search of another pumpkin.

Grant returned his attention to Jenna. He knew she was right about Hannah; it felt good to have someone to talk about his daughters with. It felt good to know he could trust Jenna's judgment when he wasn't sure he could trust his own.

"You know he asked her to the winter formal next month," Grant continued.

"I know. She already called about going shopping for a long gown. Her first formal dance."

Grant groaned as they wandered down the dirt road between the pumpkin patches. Most of the vines had died back and the ground was covered in bright-orange pumpkins of every imaginable shape and size. "They're growing up too fast," he told Jenna.

She rested her cheek on his arm. "Yesterday you said they were growing up too slowly."

"That was just because Maddy stopped up the upstairs toilet with gauze bandages again. No proper disposal in our house for post-surgery, you know."

Jenna laughed and the sound of her voice in his ears made his heart swell. Again, the word *love* popped into his thoughts. Was he in love with Jenna? Was this what it was like to be in love at almost forty years old? It certainly felt different than those first stirrings he had felt in college for Ally, and then later, as their relationship had matured. Could he trust himself to know what it was like to fall in love a second time?

Amy came running toward them, dressed in a blue sweatsuit on which Jenna had painted a black cat. Amy never walked anywhere if she could run. "Can I get a red wagon?" she begged, bouncing like Tigger. "Can I? Can I? A red wagon to pull my pumpkin."

"Sure." Jenna turned to point toward the small building in the parking lot where you paid for your pumpkins. "Right up there against that shed. See them?"

Amy bounded off in the direction of the wagons. "Be right back, Becka," she hollered. "Getting a red wagon!"

Jenna groaned aloud. "Now you want worries. There are worries." She waggled her finger, still holding on to Grant's hand. "I tried to ignore the whole Jeffery thing like you said, thinking that if I did, it would go away."

"It hasn't?"

Jenna stopped to look at an oval-shaped pumpkin along the edge of the road. Grant knew she always looked for interesting shapes for carving. While Grant and his girls always did the typical round jack-o'-lanterns, Jenna's were always the most unusual in town. She carved ghosts and goblins, leprechauns, cats and anything imaginable.

"I think it's getting worse. Amy refuses to budge on the Jeffery issue. Now she's insisting he's her boyfriend." She grabbed Grant's hand again and they continued along the dirt road.

Amy ran by them, pulling a red wagon that rattled so loudly it sounded as if it was about to lose its rusty wheels.

Jenna waited for Amy to pass before she continued. "And now she's talking about this place, Logan House, where Jeffery lives."

"Logan House? Isn't that the group home over on the bay?"

Jenna released his hand to smooth her lustrous red hair that she wore pulled into a ponytail and tied back with a black-and-white scrunchy covered in ghosts. On any other adult woman, it would have looked silly. On Jenna...it was charming.

"Apparently, the whole house is full of men and women like Amy."

"With Down's, you mean?" Grant asked.

"I guess. A couple of kids in Amy's bowling group live there. I never looked into it because I would never put Amy in a home." Her voice took on an edge that Grant didn't hear often. "I swore to my mother I wouldn't."

"Easy, easy there," Grant said. "No one said anything about putting Amy in a home. You're doing a great job taking care of her."

Jenna glanced in Amy's direction. She was helping Maddy load a pumpkin into the red wagon. Grant and Jenna stopped for a moment to watch Amy help Maddy into the wagon.

Jenna smiled sadly as Amy tucked the gorilla lovingly under Maddy's arm.

"Amy is the one talking about it. The other night she actually said she needed a vacation."

"A vacation?" Grant asked.

Jenna threw up both hands. "Oh, yes. Jeffery and his friends at Logan House are going to some amusement park in Virginia. Spending the night in a hotel. No parents. Just a chaperone from the house. Amy wanted to know if she could go, too. Can you believe that? This is all Jeffery's idea, I just know it." She frowned. "I don't even think Amy knew there was such a place before *he* told her."

Grant reached for Jenna's hand and brought it to his lips. "Jenna, you can't be upset with Amy for wanting a little independence. It's what you've worked for all these years."

Jenna stared at her sneakers. "I guess you're right. But a boyfriend?" She met Grant's eyes, her face etched with worry. "I don't know how to deal with Amy having a boyfriend. I don't know what to say to her. About kissing. About sex." She shook her head. "She doesn't even know what sex *is.*"

Grant drew Jenna into his arms and gave her a hug. "It's going to be all right. Didn't you just tell me that Hannah isn't going to do anything she shouldn't? That I raised her too well?" He grasped Jenna by the shoulders. "Well, you don't need to worry about Amy. She isn't going to do anything she shouldn't. You've raised her too well."

Jenna sighed. "I don't know, Grant. This isn't the same. Amy doesn't have the same capabilities that Hannah has, and you know it."

He brushed a wisp of hair off her face, wishing they were alone, wishing he could kiss away the worry line around her mouth. "I think Amy's more capable than you realize. Maybe more than you want her to be," he said gently.

Jenna lowered his hands and they parted. "I think we had better just agree to disagree on this one." She clapped her hands together. "So, are we pumpkin hunting or what?"

He grinned. "Okay, let's go get a pumpkin."

Jenna parted the living room curtain and watched for Grant's headlights on the street. It was a Sunday evening, unseasonably warm for the first week of November. Jenna and Grant hadn't had a moment of time alone since before Halloween and it was Jenna who had suggested that Grant come over for a walk on the beach. He had promised he would be over as soon as he tucked his younger daughters into bed. Hannah had agreed to baby-sit for an hour so Grant could get out of the house.

Jenna dropped the curtain and wandered over to the coffee table to straighten up a pile of magazines. She knew it made Grant crazy to see her house untidy, and she did make a conscious effort to straighten up before he came, but ultimately, she figured it didn't bother him too much, otherwise he wouldn't keep coming around, would he?

Full of nervous excitement at the thought of actually having a few minutes alone with Grant, she walked back to the window to watch for him. His girls were taken care of, and Amy was next door with Mrs. Cannon. They could actually focus on each other for a few minutes.

For weeks, Jenna had let things between her and Grant run their course. She tried hard not to think about where it was leading and she had certainly not brought up the subject with him. She guessed he was avoiding it as much she was. But at some point, she knew they needed to discuss the relationship that was growing between them.

What did Grant want from her other than companionship and the occasional kiss? What did she want from him? Once upon a time, she had wanted a husband, a family. After the nightmare with Paul, she had given up on the idea. And now she was almost forty.

But was she still clinging to some remnant of that

dream? Did she really think Grant would ask her to marry him?

She couldn't say yes of course. It didn't matter how she felt about him. It didn't matter that she was in love with him. There wasn't any way they could make a marriage work. Not with so many things against them. Blending a family was hard enough, but with Amy as a factor—Amy who had recently taken to mood swings and argumentative behavior—marriage just didn't seem possible. How could Jenna bring that kind of disharmony into his orderly household? How could she do that to the girls she loved as if they had come from her own body?

At the sight of headlights she recognized as Grant's coming down the street, she groaned and dropped the curtain. She knew she ought to put an end to things here and now. Just tell Grant the whole thing was getting too dangerous, that she didn't want to see anyone get hurt.

She heard the car door shut.

She wouldn't tell him that she was in love with him, of course. She would just tell him that he meant a great deal to her. That he was her best friend and that she wanted to preserve that friendship.

Grant tapped on the front door and walked into the darkness. "Jenna?"

"Here," she called from the window.

He stood there for a moment, smiling at her in a way she didn't think Paul had ever smiled at her. He lifted his hand. "Want to go for a walk? I brought a towel in case we want to sit on the beach for a few minutes.'' Grant spoke in that low, sexy voice of his that was more sensual than a tray of warm chocolate chip oatmeal cookies.

A voice that made her tingle to her toes.

''Sure,'' she said, letting him take her hand.

Maybe she'd tell him after the walk.

Hand in hand, Grant and Jenna left her cottage. They walked the two blocks to the beach and took the path through the dunes.

''Girls tucked in?'' Jenna asked, feeling oddly nervous.

''Yup.''

''Hannah find her missing jeans?''

''Yup. At a girlfriend's house.''

Jenna nodded. Grant's hand was warm in hers. ''Hey, did Becka ask you about that salt ornament recipe? I think I found it.''

Grant squeezed her hand as they crossed the soft sand and headed for the water's edge. The waves crashed just off the beach, filling the air with the scent of seawater and haunting sounds.

''Jenna,'' he said gently. ''I came over to see you to get away from them for a few minutes.'' He glanced at her in the darkness. The beach was lit only by the rising half-moon. ''I wanted to spend a few minutes alone with you.''

She chuckled. ''It's okay. I know what you mean. I...I was looking forward to being alone with you, too. Not that I don't love the girls, but—''

''But it would be nice to have a life beyond the

girls, beyond Amy, beyond the Starfish Academy,'' he said.

Grant's words seemed strangely ominous. She was afraid to ask him what he meant. This would be the opportunity to tell him what she'd rehearsed in the living room.

But it was such a perfect night. The breeze of the ocean was cool, and Grant, zipped up in his gray hooded sweatshirt, was so warm....

''Want to sit?'' he asked. ''Watch the waves?''

She nodded, hugging herself as he spread out the big towel. ''Beautiful night,'' she mused. ''I can't believe it's so warm.''

He sat down and raised his hand to her. She took it and settled beside him. He casually slipped his arm around her waist. Through her green sweatpants, she could feel the heat of his hand on her hip.

''I think I like the ocean better like this,'' she said. ''Even better than a sunny June day. It's just so incredibly beautiful.''

''Like you,'' he murmured.

Jenna wasn't expecting that. It came out of nowhere. Grant wasn't the kind of person who gushed compliments, and she wasn't the kind of person who got them often. Not compliments like that, at least.

''Grant,'' she murmured. This was it. She needed to say her piece. But when she turned to look at him, he had that look in his eyes that told her he wasn't in the mood for talking. Just one kiss, she promised herself.

He leaned forward to meet her lips, taking his time

to caress first her bottom lip and then her top. He nibbled on her lower lip, then plucked deliciously at it with his.

"Grant," she breathed.

"Jenna..."

She couldn't help herself. He tasted so good. His arms around her felt so good. She parted her lips, letting him slip his tongue into her mouth.

She melted in his arms as Grant threaded his fingers through her hair. She craved his touch and the feel of his fingertips on her cheek, craved the warmth of his body pressed against hers on the cool night.

Without consciously realizing what she was doing, she lowered herself onto her back. Or maybe he'd eased her back on the towel—she wasn't sure which.

As they fell back into the sand, his hand inadvertently brushed her breast. A moan escaped her lips.

They barely came up for air and kissed again. It was if the last week of seeing each other, but not really being alone, had built up too much need. She couldn't get enough of him and it didn't seem that he could get enough of her.

He slid his hand over her shoulder and brushed her breast. She moaned again. Even through the thickness of her T-shirt and sweatshirt, she could feel her nipple pucker in response. She curled against him, molding her body to his, feeling his muscular hardness against her soft curves.

Grant pulled away suddenly and sat up. "Jenna," he panted, trying to catch his breath. "I...I'm sorry. I...I apologize."

She sat up beside him on the towel, chuckling nervously as she straightened her sweatshirt. "It's all right," she breathed knowing she was as fully responsible as he was.

"I didn't mean—"

She pressed her cheek to his shoulder. "Grant, it's all right. Really. I..." She groaned aloud. "I wanted you to touch me," she admitted sheepishly.

For a moment he sat elbows on his knees, obviously trying to clear his head.

The wind blew, whipping her hair across her face. She pushed it away. "I think we should go back," she said shakily.

He rose and offered his hand to help her up. "I think you're right," he agreed, pulling her to her feet. "I guess next time we go for a walk, we'd better take those little chaperones with us."

She laughed with him as she grabbed up the towel. Hand in hand, they walked back up the street toward Jenna's house. As they reached her block, Jenna noticed the silhouette of two figures in the side yard.

"What the heck?"

It was two people embracing.

Jenna thought sure she recognized one of the silhouettes. It was a short and stocky female. She knew she recognized the jean jacket on the other person.

Jenna released Grant's hand and sprinted across the lawn. "Amy Marie Cartwright!"

Chapter Eight

Jenna grabbed Amy's sweatshirt and pulled her out of the shadows of the side yard into the light of the streetlamp.

"Jenna, what are you doing here? I thought you went for a walk." Amy looked as if she was going to burst into tears.

Grant came up behind Jenna. "Take a deep breath," he murmured in her ear. "They were just hugging."

Jenna wanted to shout at Amy. She wanted to grasp the jean jacket and give the young man a good push. Instead, she took a deep breath. Grant was right. Amy hadn't done anything wrong. Thank goodness he was here, or she might have done something she would have regretted later.

"Jeffery, what are you doing here?" Jenna asked, surprised by how calm she sounded.

"I...I came to see Amy, Miss Cartwright," he said bashfully. "I came to visit her."

Jenna looked at Amy. "You're supposed to be at Mrs. Cannon's."

Amy stared at the ground, twisting her hands together. "I told a fib," she confessed. "I told her I saw you outside the window. She thinks I went home with you."

Jenna had to take another breath. She was shocked by Amy's lie, but maybe even more shocked by the fact that Amy had the ability to lie and the forethought. This obviously had been planned out by Amy and Jeffery so that they could see each other alone. Amy had never done anything like this before.

Jenna felt the pressure of Grant's hand on her shoulder. "Let's go inside," he suggested quietly.

Jenna ran her hand over her head, brushing her hair from her face. "Jeffery, hon, how did you get here? Did your brother bring you?"

He shook his head. "I walked, Miss Cartwright."

"Across the highway?" Jenna asked with surprise. Route One was a busy highway with three lanes going in each direction. It wasn't safe for anyone to cross on foot in the dark.

Jeffery lowered his head.

"Does anyone know you're here?" Jenna persisted.

He didn't respond, but continued to stare at his sneakers.

Jenna took another deep breath. "Well, let's go inside. Do you know the phone number to Logan

House, Jeffery? We can call and get someone to pick you up, or I'll take you home."

He followed Jenna, rattling off the number.

Jenna let the four of them into the house. "Do you need me to call Logan House, or can you do it, Jeffery?"

"I can do it."

Jenna fetched the cordless phone for Jeffery. Out of the corner of her eye, she spotted Grant putting on some water for tea, and headed toward him, needing his strength and confidence. At the moment, she didn't have a clue as to how to handle the situation.

As Jeffery made his phone call, Jenna went to Grant in the kitchen.

"You okay?" he asked. He grabbed her hand, gave it a squeeze and then released it.

She met his gaze and her heart gave a little patter. She was amazed that after this turn of events, she could still react to his touch this way. Tonight she and Grant had come very close to crossing the line between just kissing to...more than just kissing, and she wasn't certain how she felt about that. She had fully intended to break things off with him tonight and instead, she'd ended up rolling in the sand with him. What was she going to do? She loved him. It was as simple as that. She loved him and she didn't know what she was going to do about it.

Jeffery walked into the kitchen and handed the phone to Jenna. "Thank you, Miss Cartwright. Miss Madison will be here to get me in a few minutes," he said contritely. "I told her where you live. She isn't going to walk; she's going to come in the van."

Jenna nodded. "Okay. Well, why don't you go into the living room and sit with Amy on the couch? You can wait there."

Jenna watched him go back into the kitchen and turned her attention back to Grant.

"I need to go," he said gently. "I told Hannah I wouldn't be too late. Unless you need me, of course."

She needed him all right, but not the way he meant it. It was probably just as well if he left now, anyway. She didn't think she should be alone with him any more tonight. "Go," she said. She lifted up on her toes and kissed his cheek, not trusting herself.

He turned his face to meet her lips.

It was a quick kiss, but the heat of his mouth seared hers. She would probably need a cool shower before bed tonight.

"Want me to call you when I get home?" Grant asked.

She nodded. "I think I'll be up a while." She managed a wry grin.

"I'll let myself out."

Grant took the long way home to give himself a chance to get his bearings. He didn't know what had come over him tonight. What had come over him, period. He and Ally had always had a good relationship and that included sex. But he never remembered feeling this way. Like he couldn't get enough of her, the way he couldn't get enough of Jenna. Maybe he had felt this way in the beginning with Ally, and just couldn't remember.

Thoughts of Ally brought him to the issue of the videotape. It was still in the den. If their relationship was going to go any further, he needed to tell Jenna about the tape.

That was the big question. *Was* this relationship with Jenna going to go further, and if so, how much further? Was he ready to ask the girls to accept Jenna as their new mom? After tonight, he knew he needed to make up his mind. He wasn't the kind of man who randomly slept with women, and he knew Jenna wasn't that kind of woman, either. If their relationship was going to continue in the direction it had been headed tonight on the beach, they needed to make a commitment to each other.

Grant thought about what Ally had said on the tape and he felt an incredible sense of amazement. This was exactly what Ally had wanted. He wondered how she could have known that he could fall in love with Jenna. He smiled in the darkness as he turned into his neighborhood. It took a special woman to leave a dying wish that her husband fall in love and marry again. He had always known Ally was special, but somehow this made her even more special.

So what did he do now? He loved Jenna. He knew he loved her, and he had a good idea that the feeling was mutual. He wanted to spend the rest of his life with her. He wanted to share his life with his girls, with Jenna and with Amy, too.

He wanted to ask Jenna to marry him.

But just the thought of asking her to marry him made him break out into a sweat. He was too old for wooing. He wasn't the romantic kind. He was certainly no Brad Pitt.

And what if she said no?

He turned onto his street.

Of course, how would he know if he didn't ask her? There would be no chance of them living happily ever after if he couldn't get the nerve up to tell her he loved her and ask her to marry him.

Grant signaled to turn and was surprised to see a car in his driveway. He glanced up at the front porch to see Hannah. Hannah...and her boyfriend...kissing.

Grant slammed on his breaks a little harder than he intended. He was out of the car before the engine cut off.

Either the appearance of headlights, or Grant practically running up the sidewalk caught Hannah's and the young man's attention. Hannah stepped out of Mark's embrace. He took a step backward, down the brick steps.

"Dad," Hannah said weakly, "you're home."

Grant halted at the steps and looked at the young man, whom he had met a couple of times before. Mark stuffed his hands into the pockets of his baggy jeans and slouched against the rail.

Grant hated slouching.

"Dad...um, Mark just came by to drop off my book. I left it at his house when we were studying together." She pointed lamely to the textbook that rested next to the door.

Grant gave Mark his best Daddy-of-the-girl-you-were-just-kissing glare. ‘‘Glad you could bring it by, Mark,’’ he said tightly as he walked up the steps onto the porch. ‘‘Good night.’’

Hannah took one look at Grant, gave a quick wave to her boyfriend, grabbed her book and hurried into the house. Grant closed the door behind them and flipped off the porch light. Mark could find his own way to his car in the dark. He had certainly found his way to Hannah's lips in the dark.

Hannah turned to him. ‘‘Dad, I know what you're thinking, but he just came to bring me my book.’’

Grant gestured with a pointed finger. ‘‘You know no boys are allowed in this house when I'm not home.’’

‘‘I know that. He didn't come inside. I met him on the porch.’’ Hannah's cheeks were flushed, her voice a little unsteady, but she stood her ground.

They had been kissing. Grant saw them kissing. Of course, he knew they had to be kissing. That's what fifteen- and sixteen-year-olds did. Hell, it was apparently what men and women pushing forty did, given the opportunity. But seeing that slouching boy put his arms around his little girl, his lips on hers…

Grant took a deep breath.

‘‘I didn't do anything wrong, Dad,’’ Hannah said. ‘‘It was just a good-night kiss. He hadn't been here five minutes. I swear he hadn't. We were right on the porch the whole time. You can ask nosy Mrs. Bagley across the street. She was watching us the whole time through the curtains.’’

He lifted his gaze to meet hers. He exhaled slowly. "It's okay, Hannah. I'm just having a little parental crisis here. Little girls aren't supposed to grow up to be young women."

She looked at him the way she did when she didn't quite understand him.

"It's okay. I'll work my way through this. You go on to bed," he said with a half smile. "Thanks for watching your sisters. Put it on my tab."

She stood there for a second, looking at him with an expression that made his heart ache. Grant took an awkward step forward, wrapped Hannah in his arms and hugged her tightly. She smelled of big-girl things like hair gel and lip gloss, but when he closed his eyes, she still smelled like his little girl. He kissed the top of her head and fought the lump in his throat.

"I love you, Daddy," she whispered. She gave him a quick, soft peck on the cheek and then bounded up the stairs before he could react.

"Love you, too, Hannah Banana," he murmured, swallowing the lump in his throat. Hannah really was growing up into a fine young lady.

Grant walked into the dark kitchen to get the phone. Jenna answered on the second ring.

"Hey," she said.

He smiled. "Hey." He walked down the hall without turning on any lights and went into the den. He sat down in his chair. He liked talking to Jenna in the dark like this. It made him feel as if she were here in the darkness with him.

"Jeffery gone?"

"Someone from Logan House came and picked him up just a minute ago. Madison someone. She was very nice. Very apologetic. Jeffery is not supposed to leave without letting someone know, and he is not supposed to be crossing the highway alone."

"How's Amy?"

Jenna sighed. "Upset."

"For what they were doing or because you caught her?"

To his relief, Jenna laughed. "I'm not sure if she knows."

"Well, if it makes you feel any better," Grant said, "there must have been something in the air tonight. I came home to find Hannah on the porch in a lip lock with Mark."

"Oh, no."

"It's okay. She didn't let him in to the house or anything. As she had to point out to me, she didn't do anything wrong. He just dropped off a book." He wanted to say that he couldn't really chastise Hannah, not after his own behavior tonight, but he wasn't quite sure how to say it.

"Well," Jenna said, "it's not like either of us can say much." She gave a throaty laugh and he knew she was thinking the very same thing he was.

Again, he smiled. "Just for the record, tonight was wonderful. It's gotten me thinking."

She was quiet on the other end of the phone.

"But we can talk later," he said quickly. He tried to tell himself he wasn't getting cold feet. He couldn't just jump into a conversation about marriage. He had to have a plan. He had to have a ring. Every man who wanted to ask a woman to marry him had to have a plan and a ring. "I'll let you go," he continued. "I just wanted to say good-night."

"Good night. Talk to you tomorrow," she murmured.

Grant hung up the phone and sat there in the dark for a minute. Just talking to Jenna made his pulse quicken. He really was in love with her. The thought made him smile. After Ally died, he had been afraid he would never be happy again.

He got up and turned on the light. Come to think of it, it had been Jenna who had understood those feelings. It had been Jenna who told him he would have to give himself time.

Grant set down the phone and went to the videotapes arranged in alphabetical order on a shelf in the entertainment nook. He kept his own video collection of old movies and documentaries separate from the kids' Disney video collection. At the end of the tapes were several that were unmarked. He grabbed the one that he knew was Ally's and popped it into the VCR. He would watch it one more time and then he would box it up and put it in the attic.

He walked back to his favorite plaid chair, sat down and picked up the remote. He'd watch Ally one last time and then he would tell her goodbye. It was the only way, he knew, that he could truly bring Jenna into his life.

With a touch of sadness, Grant hit Play on the remote. As Ally's smiling face appeared on the screen, he smiled, too.

Thanks to his sweet, practical Ally, life was going to be good again.

Chapter Nine

Jenna nervously smoothed her skirt and glanced at the clock in the kitchen. It was 8:58; Grant would be here in less than a minute. He was never late.

She walked down the hall and pushed Amy's door open a bit. By the glow of the night-light, she could see her sister asleep beneath her Beauty and the Beast bedspread. She looked so sweet when she was asleep. So beautiful. Asleep this way, Jenna couldn't see the anger she had seen lately in Amy's eyes. The resentment.

After last week's little episode in the side yard, Jenna had called Logan House and made it clear to the director that Jeffery was not to visit unannounced again. Amy had been furious with Jenna and had gone two days without talking to her before finally giving in over a big bowl of ice cream. Jenna had tried to explain to Amy that she wasn't trying to keep Amy from seeing Jeffrey, but was just looking out for her best interest. She could see Jeffery every Saturday at bowling, for the rest of her life if she wanted to.

Jenna closed the door quietly so as not to wake her sister. Now Amy lived for Saturdays.

There was a tap on the front door. Grant was here. He had asked if he could come over for a few minutes after the girls went to bed. He said he needed to talk to her.

Jenna didn't know how she felt about being alone with Grant like this. After the beach incident last weekend, she wasn't certain she trusted herself, or her emotions. But Grant said he really needed to talk to her, and she couldn't turn him down.

Grant walked into the house, still wearing his suit from work, his tie cinched to his neck. Jenna had to smile; she had shed her panty hose and tight shoes hours ago.

"Hi, there." She pressed her hand to his lapel and gave him a quick kiss. He had put on fresh cologne before coming over. Something was definitely up.

"Hi, there." His mouth lingered over hers for just a second too long, and she took a step back, amazed by how quickly he could flip her switches these days. "You want to sit down?" She indicated the couch where she'd swept off piles of newspaper only a few minutes before.

"Actually..." He glanced in the direction of the back porch. "It's such a nice night out, I thought we could sit in your garden. I don't think it will be too cold, sheltered by the fence."

Jenna couldn't resist a smile. He was such a sweetie. He knew how much she loved her garden, even in the fall and winter. He knew how much she enjoyed sharing it with others.

"Sure. That would be great. Just let me grab my jacket."

When she returned from her bedroom, Grant was gone from the living room. The door that led from the glassed-in back porch to her garden was ajar.

How strange that he didn't wait for her. But then he'd been acting strangely all week. Since their "beach date" last weekend he had seemed different, more upbeat, and happier. But, he'd also been secretive. The way her kindergartners were when their birthday or Christmas was coming up.

He had piqued her curiosity. She had been so busy worrying over Amy and Jeffery that she hadn't really had a lot of time to talk to Grant this week. She threw on her jacket and walked out into the garden. What did he want to talk to her about? What was so important?

She spotted Grant near the little stone bench on the far side of the garden. He was patting his suit pockets, looking for something as he talked to himself. What was this man up to, mumbling to himself, acting all nervous?

She halted in the middle of the stone path, raising her hand to her mouth. Grant was here at night, dressed in his suit. He had wanted to take her into the garden, which was so romantic.

Romantic? Surely, he wasn't going to—

Suddenly Jenna couldn't breathe.

He hadn't even told her he loved her.

Was Grant going to ask her to marry him?

She turned her back to him, her hands trembling with excitement or fear—she didn't know which.

What was she going to do? She didn't want to hurt Grant, but could she marry him? Would it be fair to him, to his girls, to Amy?

"There you are," Grant called.

Jenna spun around. Caught. She wanted to run. She wanted to hide. She wanted to fling herself into his arms.

"Come sit here," he said, offering his hand. "Sit with me on the bench." He looked up into the sky. "Look how bright the stars are. We won't get too many more nice nights like this for a while, will we?"

She couldn't resist. She was powerless to resist his warm, sexy voice, his beckoning hand. Slowly Jenna walked down the stone path to where he waited.

Grant wrapped his arm around her waist as they sat beside each other, silent for a moment. Jenna struggled to keep her heart beating steadily. Grant seemed to be trying to find his voice. He began to pat his coat pockets again.

"Jenna." He took a breath. He was as nervous as she had ever seen him. More nervous than he had been that moment in the chapel before he walked out to wait for Ally on their wedding day. More nervous than when he had waited at Admitting to get Ally a bed the day Hannah was born.

"Jenna, I've rehearsed what I want to say and—"

"Grant, you—"

He grabbed her hand. "Please, Jenna, just let me speak. Let me get this all out before I forget something, or worse, fall over in a dead faint, crack my skull on your stepping stones and force you to call an ambulance."

She laughed and it made her feel better. She could breathe again. Grant was beside her, sweet Grant. Grant, the man she loved whether she wanted to love him or not.

"I've been thinking a lot, especially this last week." He turned to her, taking her hands in his.

She could see his face in the shadows cast by the dim glow of stars and the background light from the house across the garden. She could feel, not only the warmth of his hands wrapped around hers, but also the warmth of his body, the warmth of his heart. She could hear the sounds of the waves crashing on the beach in the distance.

"Jenna...Jenna the fact is that..." His words came out in a rush. "That I'm in love with you."

She felt her heart soar. She didn't want to go there. Didn't want to take the chance of getting hurt again, but he was taking her there anyway. Grant loved her. He loved her!

"And I think you love me, too." He bit down on his lower lip. "And I know maybe we didn't expect this to happen. But, I want to spend the rest of my life with you. I..." He took a deep breath. "Jenna, will you marry me? Will you be my wife? Will you be my lover and the mother of my children?"

Tears filled Jenna's eyes. When she looked in his warm brown eyes, there was only one response she could make.

''Yes,'' she breathed. ''I love you, Grant, and I will marry you.''

He held her gaze and in an instant, his nervousness seemed to slip away.

''Jenna,'' he whispered. He pulled her close and kissed her and then began to fumble in his pockets again.

She was laughing and crying at the same time.

Finally, from his inside suit pocket, he produced a tiny velvet box. ''Now you can have whatever you want, but I found this in an antique shop and thought it was perfect.''

He opened the box and the ring she saw nestled in the black velvet took her breath away. It was a 1920s-style platinum-and-diamond ring. It was the most beautiful ring she had ever seen in her life.

''Oh, it's beautiful,'' she breathed.

''Not as beautiful as you are.'' Grant took the ring from the box, lifted her left hand and slipped it on her finger.

Jenna threw her arms around him. ''Grant I don't know what to say. This is so unexpected. All of it. I never thought—''

''That either of us would be this happy,'' he finished for her. He was now calm, his voice warm and full of emotion. ''Never thought either of us would love again.''

She nodded, knowing he above all others understood. She had loved Paul so much, and yet she had lost him just as Grant had lost Ally. He understood the heartache. He knew how hard it had been to go on.

"So you'll marry me?" he asked again.

She held out her hand to look at the antique engagement ring, nodding frantically. She was so happy she thought she would burst inside. Gone was every bit of logic, of sensibility, she had. All that mattered at this moment was that Grant loved her and wanted to marry her.

"You sure?" he whispered. He seemed to be as disbelieving of the whole situation as she was.

Jenna grabbed Grant by his red tie and pulled him close enough to touch his nose with hers. "Come here," she whispered, "and let me you show you how sure I am."

He took her mouth hungrily. Jenna slid her hands up and over his broad shoulders. He slipped his hands around her waist and pulled her onto his lap.

Jenna wished the kiss could last forever. He made her hot and cold at the same time. The warmth of his arms around her waist and the taste of his mouth on hers made her heart pound and her head swim.

Grant pulled away first. "Jenna," he murmured, panting. "I think we need to marry soon."

She laughed, her voice shaky on the cool night air. "You do?"

He nodded, still struggling to catch his breath. "Because I don't know how long I can control myself." He held her gaze with his as he smoothed back a loose lock of her hair. "Because I want so badly to make love with you."

"But we should be married...for the girls' sake," she said, not sure if she believed that right now. It would have been so easy to walk into the house, into her bedroom and shut the door.

"No," he murmured, surprising her with his answer. "For *our* sake. If we're going to make this commitment to each other, to love and cherish one another for the rest of our lives, I think we need to wait. It should be a part of the package. We make this vow to each other before God, and holding each other naked every night is the bonus." He grinned.

It was probably the sweetest thing he had ever said to her. Who said chivalry and romance were dead?

Grant kissed her again, but this time it was a gentle kiss...a kiss of promise. Of anticipation of things to come.

"I'd better go," he whispered, easing her off his lap and rising to his feet. "Before I change my mind and carry you into the house."

Jenna just stood there in the middle of the fall, nighttime garden, smiling as he walked out the back gate. Against all sense, she couldn't stop smiling.

Grant got up the following morning before the girls. He fried bacon and then mixed up a veggie omelette. His daughters loved breakfast and they loved veggie omelettes.

Becka was the first one down the stairs. "Oooh,

bacon on a school morning?'' She snatched a piece off the plate from the counter. ''I'll get the juice.''

Maddy appeared next, dressed in her school uniform of a jumper and turtleneck and navy tights...with her bunny slippers on her feet. Grant kissed the top of her tousled head as she walked sleepily to her chair at the kitchen table.

''Eggs and bacon coming up,'' Grant said cheerfully. He felt good this morning. Amazingly good. He knew he had done the right thing in asking Jenna to marry him. He knew she would be a good mother to his girls, and he knew she would make him happy. She had already made him happier than he had ever imagined he would be again.

Hannah was the last one downstairs. She dropped her book bag in the hallway. ''Wow, Dad, eggs and bacon on a school day.''

''Toast, too,'' Maddy piped up.

Hannah slid into her chair across from her father's as Grant put the plate of eggs onto the table and took his own seat.

''So what's up, Dad? Some special occasion?'' Hannah asked, reaching for the omelet to give Maddy a portion.

Grant sat erect at the head of the table, hands planted on both sides of his plate. He took a deep breath. Suddenly he was nervous again. He knew the girls loved Jenna. He knew they would be thrilled that he was going to marry her, and that she was going to move in. But he still felt strange. This would be the first time he told anyone about him and Jenna. ''Actually, this is a special occasion.'' He looked from one daughter to the next. ''I have some big news, and I can't think of anyone I'd rather share it with first than you guys.''

''We're getting a puppy?'' Maddy asked, her mouth full of eggs.

Becka rolled her eyes.

''No, Maddy. I told you. No puppy,'' Grant said.

''We're moving to Tahiti,'' Becka suggested. She had just written a report for school on Tahiti and had asked Grant the previous evening if they could all move there.

Maddy giggled.

''Girls!'' Grant was losing his equilibrium. He had already practiced what he was going to say, but he needed to hurry up and say it.

''Let Dad talk, you two chatterboxes.'' Hannah looked at her dad. ''Tell us.''

Grant took a deep breath. ''Well, you know Jenna and I have been dating…and…'' His whole rehearsed speech was gone from his head. But he had to go on. His daughters were all waiting.

''And, Jenna and I have realized we're in love with each other, and I asked her to marry me.''

Maddy's face lit up. ''Aunt Jenna is going to be my mommy?'' she squealed with delight. ''Then I'll always have enough bandages for my animals.''

Becka was smiling. Nodding. Trying to play cool, but Grant could tell by the look on her face that she was happy. ''My dad's getting married to my aunt Jenna.'' She nodded again. ''Too bad we don't still have show-and-tell in school any more. I'd win for sure.''

Grant could feel the tightness in his neck falling away. It was going to be okay. Everything was going to be fine. Then he shifted his gaze to Hannah.

His relief was a little premature.

Hannah looked as if she was either going to burst into tears or throw her plate of eggs at him. She pressed her hands to the table with such pressure that he thought the legs might snap off. ''Dad...how could you?'' she whispered.

Before he could answer, she jumped out of her chair. ''How could you?'' she shouted.

And ran from the kitchen.

Chapter Ten

Maddy's eyes widened with shock in reaction to her sister's outburst. Then her mouth puckered and a fat tear ran down her face.

"Drama Queen," Becka muttered as she leaned over to give her little sister a hug.

Grant lunged out of his chair. His first reaction was one of anger. Hannah's behavior was completely inappropriate. But then he forced himself to remain calm, reminding himself of what a big change this would be to Hannah, to the whole family.

"It's okay, sweetie," Grant said, giving Maddy a kiss on the top of her head. "Hannah's just upset. Daddy will go talk to her. You eat your breakfast." His gaze met Becka's, and he knew Becka realized he needed her to take care of Maddy for a minute.

Grant walked out of the kitchen. Hannah's bedroom door slammed as he started up the staircase. At her door, he knocked.

"Go away!" she shouted.

"Hannah, I need to talk to you." Grant was torn by emotion. This reaction took him completely by surprise. Hannah had been so supportive of him dating Jenna. She had actually remarked that they looked "cute" holding hands.

When Hannah didn't respond, he opened her door. "Hannah, you need to tell me why you're upset."

She lay prone on her bed, her face in her pillow. She lifted her head. Her face was already puffy and red from crying. "Why I'm upset? Because you just said you're getting a new wife."

"But Hannah, you love Jenna." He moved to the edge of her bed and sat down. "If I recall correctly, you were the one who said you thought I ought to take her out."

"I said go out on a date. I didn't say marry her," she retorted.

Grant looked away, not sure what to say now. "Hannah, I know this is going to mean change in our family, but believe me, it's going to mean good changes. I'm trying, but I can't keep everything together here. As a team, Jenna and I will be able to do more with you girls. Spend more time with you."

"Go away," she muttered from her pillow. "I don't want to talk about it."

Grant laid his hand on her back and rubbed it through her lime green sweatshirt. He debated whether or not to continue this conversation. In the end, he decided that maybe it was best to give her a little time and then talk about it later.

"Hannah, I need to get ready to go to work. You go to school and we'll talk about this tonight, okay?"

She lifted her tear-stained face from the pillow. "Is anything I say going to change your mind about marrying her?"

He thought a moment and then met his daughter's eyes. "No," he said softly. "I love her and I want her to be my wife. I want her to help me raise you girls. I want to be her partner in caring for Amy. Now, I understand that Jenna could never replace your mother. Jenna understands that, too. But she does love you and your sisters and, Hannah, she loves me." He shook his head. "I'm sorry if this hurts you, but, Hannah, Jenna and I are getting married, and probably very soon."

Hannah buried her face in the pillow again.

Grant rose slowly. She was tearing his heart in pieces. But he had been a father long enough to know that children could not make decisions for adults. He also knew Hannah well enough to realize that her outlook on life was very mature most of the time. She had a right to act her age once in a while.

He kissed the top of her head and left her alone, closing her door quietly behind him.

It was going to be a long day.

Grant didn't get a chance to speak to Jenna alone until after lunch. Last night after he proposed to her and got home, an overwhelming sense of guilt had washed over him. He had packed Ally's tape away in a cardboard box to carry up to the attic. He had fully intended to tell Jenna about the tape, but then he got carried away with the whole idea of asking her to marry him. Buying the ring. Practicing what he would say. Then he had proposed, and it hadn't seemed right to tell her then.

But he needed to tell her now. He needed to tell her right away. He knew it wouldn't change anything between them. He loved her because...because he did. Not because Ally had told him to fall in love with her. But Jenna had a right to know about the tape just the same.

Grant slipped into Jenna's classroom. He hated having to tell her here, but in person was better than on the phone, and both of them were so busy that he honestly didn't know when he would see her again on a real date.

Jenna's class was gone, and she was seated at her desk shelling an ear of corn into a Tupperware bowl. "What are you doing?" he asked.

She smiled up him. "Shelling corn to grind to make corn meal to make corn bread."

From the doorway, Grant glanced into the hall. No one saw him come in. Everyone in the school knew they were dating, but he and Jenna had tried hard to keep their professional and personal lives separate.

He closed her classroom door. "I told the girls this morning," he said, thinking he would ease into the "Ally's Videotape" conversation.

She continued to shell corn. "And?"

"Maddy and Becka are thrilled."

She stopped shelling corn, the sunny smile fading. "But?"

He ran his finger inside his collar, loosening it a bit. "Let's just say my teenager was less than receptive to the idea."

She rose from behind her desk. She was wearing a close-fitting thin sweater that brought attention to her breasts.

Grant didn't remember noticing before he viewed the tape in September what nice breasts she had. He had to force himself to lift his gaze to her face.

"Oh, Grant. I'm sorry." She bit down on her lower lip. "Maybe we should slow things down a little. Give her time to get used to the idea."

He shook his head. "No. I've thought about this and I think we need to go ahead and pick a date. Maybe over Christmas vacation. Easter at the latest." He looked down at his polished black dress shoes. "I think she'll come around, but honestly..."

He lifted his gaze to meet hers again and wished he could pull her into his arms right now. He could have used a hug. "This is not up to Hannah. It's up to you and me."

"All right. Whatever you think," Jenna agreed.

"What about Amy? Did you tell her?"

Jenna sat down again and reached for the ear of corn. "Talk about surprise. She barely said a word. She just went on eating her Rice Krispies." She began shelling the corn into the bowl. "I'm not sure she even understands what being married means. I told her that we would probably be moving in with you and the girls.''

''And she didn't have a problem with that?''

''I really don't know. The only thing she asked was would she have to miss bowling if the wedding was on a Saturday.''

Grant had to laugh. He glanced at his watch. He had to go. He knew the teachers were already buzzing with gossip, he didn't want to fuel the fire. He really did want to tell Jenna about the tape, but this didn't seem like the right time now.

''Well, you pick a wedding date that won't interfere with Amy's bowling.'' He walked to the door. ''You tell me where to be and when and I'll be there.''

She smiled that smile that somehow made him think of warm chocolate chip cookies and sex at the same time. ''You'd better be there,'' she called after him.

Wouldn't miss it for the world, he thought, grinning as he walked out of the classroom and down the hallway...the videotape forgotten.

Jenna finished the dinner dishes, dried her hands, and put on a kettle for tea water. She had work to do for school, but wanted to check on Amy first. Since she told Amy a week ago about hers and Grant's engagement, Amy had been strangely quiet.

Jenna walked into the hall and poked her head into Amy's bedroom. ''Hey, whatcha doing?''

Amy glanced up from her bed where she lay turning the pages of a magazine that featured monster trucks. She had already gotten ready for bed and was waiting for Jenna to tuck her in. Jenna hadn't bought the magazine for Amy, but she could guess who had.

When Amy made no reply, Jenna tried again. "What are you looking at?" She walked into the room and picked up a dirty pair of sweatpants to place in the clothes hamper. "Trucks?"

"Leave those on the floor," Amy said. "I can pick them up myself. I don't need you to clean up my clothes."

Jenna let the sweatpants slip from her fingers and fall to the carpet. She tried not to feel hurt. It was so unlike Amy to snap at her, to snap at anyone. "I'm sorry. You're right." She lifted her hands in surrender. "I have no right to come in here and touch your things."

Amy glanced at the magazine in front of her. She was lying stretched out on her bed, dressed in flannel pj's. She stared at the magazine, but she wasn't really looking at it. "I want to go to Logan House," she blurted out suddenly.

Jenna stared at her sister, wondering where on earth that had come from. "Well, maybe you could visit Jeffery some time," she stumbled. "We could go for a visit together. Maybe have hot chocolate with marshmallows. I bet Jeffery likes marshmallows just like you do."

Amy continued to stare at the monster truck on the glossy page. "I don't want to visit at Logan House." She thrust out her lower lip the way she did when she was really getting ready to dig in and refuse to do something like take a shower or clean up a mess she made. "I want to live at Logan House—without you," she added.

Jenna was floored. For a moment, she didn't know what to say. It was out of the question, of course. Amy was her responsibility. Amy would always have a home with her. She had promised their mother.

But instead of flat-out refusing her, she sat down on the edge of her bed. "Amy, what brought this on? Is this something Jeffery said?"

"No." Amy chewed nervously on the inside of her mouth. "Well, kind of maybe."

Jenna sighed. She didn't want to forbid Amy to see her friend, but this young man was obviously a bad influence. Instead, she tried a different tack. "Amy, why would you want to live there? You and I are going to move to Grant's house and live with Grant and Hannah and Becka and Maddy. Won't that be fun?"

She flipped a page in the magazine. "On my happy birthday I will be twenty-seven years old. I'm too big to live with my sister. Jeffery doesn't live with his brother anymore." She looked at Jenna, her eyes filled with what looked like resentment. "You think I can't take care of myself, but I can!"

Jenna had to look away and take a deep breath. She didn't blame Amy for this behavior. But she did blame Jeffery. Of course, when Amy got like this, there was no budging her. Like Grant had done with

Hannah, this conversation was obviously going to have to be tabled until Amy calmed down.

"Well, it's time for bed." She rose from the bed and walked to the bookshelf. "Want me to read *Inside, Outside, Upside Down* to you before you shut out the light?"

Amy stared at the magazine. "No, thank you."

Jenna paused at the door.

"Good night," Amy said.

It was an obvious dismissal. Jenna had no choice but to go.

A couple of days later, Jenna ducked into a coffee shop after school just to see Grant for a few minutes. They both had a million things to do and couldn't see each other until the weekend. He was already waiting for her.

"Hi, ya." She kissed him on the mouth and slid into the chair across from him.

"Hi, ya, yourself. I ordered you a coffee latte with extra milk."

"Just the way I like it." She smiled and slid her hand across the table to take his. "Just the way I like you." In the last few days, Jenna felt as if she was leading a fairy-tale life. Her prince had finally come for her, and this prince was definitely no frog.

"Did you pick up Hannah's gown from the shop?" she asked.

"It's in the car. You're sure you don't mind hemming it?"

"I'm sure." Jenna held his gaze. She knew how

hard this must be for him. Hannah, going to her first formal dance. Hannah, with her boyfriend. Hannah, putting up a fuss about the marriage.

"So have you gotten anywhere with her?" she asked.

"Not any further than you've gotten convincing Amy that she may not move out to live with her boyfriend."

Jenna slid her hands back to give the waitress room as she unloaded her tray with the latte, Grant's black coffee and a small plate of shortbread cookies cut in autumn shapes.

"Perfect." Jenna closed her hands around the delicate white mug, enjoying the warmth of the china and the heavenly scent of the latte. "So neither Hannah nor Amy are talking to us. I probably shouldn't ask them about being in the wedding quite yet, then, should I?"

He chuckled. "I think I would hold off on that a few days." He sipped his coffee. "But I wouldn't hold off on picking a date. I mean that, Jenna. I want you to pick a date for the wedding. You tell me what I need to do. We'll divide all of the jobs. I can get the church, find a place for a reception. Whatever you want. I'm anxious to marry you."

She smiled slyly over the edge of her coffee cup. "You're not anxious to marry me," she said softly, enjoying the flirtation. "You're just anxious to get me naked in bed."

They laughed together as he reached out to take her hands in his. He lifted them to his mouth and kissed her knuckles. ''You bet I am.'' He let go of her hands and reached for his coffee. ''Now back to life. Said boyfriend is picking Hannah up next Saturday night at six-thirty for dinner. Becka's violin recital is at three. We can do dinner afterward if you want.''

''And maybe squeeze in a minute or two alone?''

He lifted an eyebrow, giving her a lascivious look. ''If you think you can be safely alone with me.''

She laughed again. ''You're right. We'd better hurry up and get married.'' She leaned forward, lowering her voice to whisper something when the shop door opened, its bell jingling.

''Dad. There you are. I thought I saw your car.''

Jenna sat back on the bench and turned to see Hannah coming toward them.

''I saw your car out front. I just wanted to see if it was okay if I go back to school to work on the dance decorations.'' Hannah halted beside the table.

Grant looked at Hannah, then at Jenna, then back at Hannah. ''Maybe. A hello, Jenna, or something equally polite, Miss Height of Rudeness.''

Hannah slouched in her best ''Mark'' imitation. She rolled her eyes. ''Hello, Jenna.''

Jenna didn't take offense. ''Hello, Hannah.''

Hannah turned back to her father, presenting her back to Jenna. ''Is it okay? Becka will get off the bus with Maddy, and I'm *assuming* you are on your way home from work.''

''You *assume* correctly,'' Grant responded.

Jenna was impressed by how well Grant handled

his teenage daughter when she ''was in a mood'' as he called it. He was his kind, loving self, as always, but he didn't wimp out. He had certain expectations from his daughter regarding respect for him and for others, and that line of respect was not to be crossed.

''I just had to stop and get your gown.'' Grant picked up his coffee. ''You can stay until six and then come home.''

''But, Dad—''

''Six o'clock and then you come home,'' he repeated firmly. ''You've been spending too much time out on school nights. Catch a ride with one of the girls, not Mark, or call me.''

Hannah stood there for a moment, then stormed out of the coffee shop. Grant looked at Jenna. ''I'm sorry.''

She reached out and touched his hand. ''It's all right. She'll come around. I know she loves me. Maybe as much as I love her.'' She offered him a reassuring smile and then turned to dig in her knapsack. ''So, you want to see what I picked for a gown, or do you want to be surprised?''

''I want to see the gown, but I'll still be surprised,'' he murmured, his dark eyes filled with warmth.

Definitely not a frog.

Chapter Eleven

Jenna gave the porch swing a push and then lifted her feet as it glided forward again, gazing over the dark lawn as she waited for Grant to come back out with the tea. She was so happy, she was afraid she was dreaming.

Grant had a scheduled church meeting for this evening so she had not thought she would be able to see him tonight. But when the meeting was cancelled at the last moment, he called her to invite her and Amy over for dinner. Despite Hannah's coolness toward her, the family dinner had been a nice one. She thought Hannah was coming around and Amy seemed content, at least for a while. Tonight, sitting at the dining room table beside Grant, holding hands as they said grace, Jenna could picture her life here in the old rambling Victorian. She could picture herself caring for the girls and Amy. She could see herself growing old with Grant.

The front screen door opened and banged shut as Grant approached carrying a tray with a teapot and two mugs on it. He had actually gone to the kitchen store and bought a teapot so that he could make her tea. Who wouldn't love this man?

"I have to say," she told him, "I like the idea of marrying a man who is a homemaker."

He glanced at her as he set the tray on a small wicker table nearby. "Just as long as you don't think that's all I'm good for." His voice was low and sexy.

He didn't have to say anything for her to understand the insinuation. The sexual tension between them now crackled each time they were together, giving Jenna a delicious sense of anticipation. She still hadn't chosen a wedding date, but she was working on it. They had an appointment with their church pastor next week, but she was leaning toward Grant's idea and marrying the week between Christmas and New Year's. In a way that seemed sudden, but when she took into account the fact that they had known each other since college, it didn't seem so. She knew Grant better than she knew herself. At least she knew most things about him. His ardor had been a pleasant surprise.

Grant left the tea to steep and caught the swing as it glided forward. He sat beside her and gave it a push. "Brrr. It's chilly out here."

"Not under here, it's not." She offered the edge of the knitted afghan she wore around her shoulders.

Ally had made it, but that didn't bother Jenna. She felt no sense of competition between herself and Ally. In a way, she found the reminders of Ally comforting. After all, she had loved Ally, too. "Want to join me?"

His smile was the only answer she needed.

Snuggled beneath the blanket, Jenna rested her head on Grant's shoulder and let him push the swing.

"Girls okay?" she asked.

"Watching a movie."

"Hannah, too?"

"Begrudgingly. Mark is busy tonight, so I guess she figured if she was stuck with us, she might as well make the best of things."

Jenna ran her hand up his arm. He was wearing a fisherman's cable-knit sweater and blue jeans. She liked this casual side of him that still had a neat air about it. "Don't worry. She'll be fine. You'd be more worried if she'd just said, 'Great, you're replacing my mother with my aunt Jenna.'"

He slid his arm around Jenna's shoulders and pulled the afghan tighter around them. "I told her I knew her mother couldn't be replaced and that had never been my intention. I told her that she could go right on calling you Aunt Jenna."

"Give her time. She'll be fine. It's just a lot to take in. It's been an eventful fall, and I think she's nervous about the dance next weekend."

Grant turned to her. "Thanks for being so understanding." He brushed his lips against hers.

Jenna let her eyes drift shut. "You're welcome."

Grant pulled back. She could tell he was trying to mind his p's and q's tonight. The kids were just inside the house. This was not the night to get all hot and bothered again.

''So how are things going with Amy?'' he asked.

Jenna exhaled. ''Honestly, I'm not sure. She just seems different to me.''

''She still likes work?''

Jenna nodded. ''Loves it.''

''Well, that's good because Starfish Academy loves her. Jean says she's a hard worker. She says she can always count on Amy to do more than she's asked.''

''No, it's not work. She just seems less content with her life than she once did. I don't know. The whole thing with Jeffery—I mean, a boyfriend? I didn't know she knew what that meant. And where did she learn to kiss?''

Grant teasingly nuzzled her neck. ''I don't know, where did any of us learn to kiss?''

He ran his warm lips over her skin sending goose bumps of pleasure through her. ''I think it's instinct,'' he said.

She laughed and pushed him away. ''I'd say your instincts are running pretty strong these days.''

He grinned in a boyish way that she never recalled seeing before. There was so much more to Grant than she had ever realized. She knew him so well, yet, he was still surprising her, and that was a good thing. Surprise was good in a marriage.

After the initial shock of realizing she had agreed to marry Grant, Jenna had begun to worry about the day-to-day grind. Grant was so neat, so organized and she…well, she just wasn't. She wondered how they would be able to live together. To work together. To raise a family together. She knew her untidiness and her tardiness annoyed him. She was sure she could make some changes to accommodate him. But she couldn't change who she was any more than she could expect him to change.

Sitting here tonight on a cool fall evening, talking like this, made Jenna think she could do this. They could do this. They could raise this family the way they wanted to see them raised, and still find personal happiness and fulfillment.

Jenna slid her hand under the afghan to take Grant's. "Everything is going to be okay, isn't it?" she asked.

He turned to her. "Of course it is." He gave a little laugh. "What makes you ask?"

She shrugged.

"Not getting cold feet already, are you?" He squeezed her hand.

She met his gaze. "Of course not. I just…I'm just beginning to realize what a monumental task we're embarking on. This isn't going to be easy. Amy is not going to be as easy to deal with as we thought she was and now Hannah—"

"Jenna, I love you," Grant said softly. "And you love me. Don't worry about Hannah or Amy. We'll work this out. I'll make it work."

She smiled. Of course, Grant would make this

work. He was a take-charge kind of guy. Mr. Organization. If he couldn't make it work, no one could.

She nodded. "You're right. Everything is going to be okay."

"It's going to be better than okay," he insisted, pressing his lips to hers. "Just wait and see."

Friday evening, Jenna sat at the kitchen table hemming Hannah's gown while Grant made dinner. The kitchen was filled with the tantalizing aroma of baked chicken.

"We're almost ready to eat," Grant called.

Amy, Becka and Maddy were in the living room listening to CDs and dancing. Hannah wasn't home from school yet. She had stayed to work on last-minute decorations for tomorrow night's dance.

"Are we going to wait for Hannah?" Jenna asked, biting the thread.

"Nah. She should be home soon, but we can eat without her if she isn't." Grant slid a tray of refrigerator biscuits into the oven. "Then I'll have to get going. I have to drop Becka off at a friend's for a sleepover and run by Chad Elder's house. He's going to be helping me with the finances on that new playground we're trying to get built in the park."

Jenna nodded. She was impressed that, even after Ally died, he had been able to not only keep up at work, but still contribute to the church they attended and the community they lived in. As Miss Oberton had recently pointed out to Jenna, "Dr. Monroe is quite a catch."

"Amy, Becka, Maddy, is the table set?"

"Set, Dad," Becka shouted above the music in the living room.

The back door banged open and Hannah walked in. Her face was red from crying.

Jenna looked from Grant to Hannah. "Hannah, what's wrong, sweetie?"

Hannah walked by the table without looking at Jenna. "You can forget the dress," she snapped. "I'm not going."

"Not going? Why not?" Jenna asked.

"I'm going to my room," Hannah told her father. "I don't want any dinner."

Grant put down the hot mitts he held in his hands and followed Hannah. Jenna wanted to go with him, but she knew it wasn't a good idea. Obviously, something had happened, and obviously, Hannah didn't want to share it with Jenna. She tried not to feel hurt.

"I'll put dinner on the table, Grant," Jenna said, getting up from the table. "You go see what's up."

Grant followed Hannah up the stairs. "What's the matter? Why aren't you going to the dance?"

"Because I'm not going anywhere with that jerk," she flung over her shoulder, running up the steps. "Okay?"

Grant calmly followed behind her. Hannah didn't often throw temper tantrums, but when she did, they were doozies. "He bail out on you, Hannah?"

She walked into her bedroom but didn't slam the door in his face. Grant knew that was as good an invitation as he was going to get.

"Oh, no," she said throwing her book bag onto her bed. "He still wants to go with me. He already spent ten bucks on a corsage, you know."

"So what's the problem? Why don't you want to go? You've worked so hard on the decorations and your gown is beautiful."

She flopped into a chair and flipped a switch to boot up her computer. "I'm not going with him because he's an ass," she said.

Ordinarily, Grant didn't tolerate bad language, but he knew how and when to pick his fights. Hannah was obviously upset and obviously hurt. "Don't you want to tell me what happened?" He stood back from her a little, knowing that at times like this she needed her space.

"I caught him kissing Brittany Anderson in the hallway when he was supposed to be getting more construction paper from the art room, that's what happened."

She didn't turn to look at him, but he knew she was crying again. He lowered his head a moment. The hardest thing he found about being a parent was not being able to protect his daughters from the hurts of the world. "Ass," he muttered.

"That's just what I thought," she said, still keeping her back to him.

Grant took another step back. He knew there wasn't much he was going to be able to do for Hannah. Not much he could say, at least not now. She was hurting and needed some time. "I'm sorry, sweetie," he said, knowing there was no sense in telling her there would be other boyfriends, and, unfortunately, other broken hearts. ''I'll save you some dinner. Maybe you'll feel like eating later.''

She signed onto the Internet and the electronic sounds filled her bedroom. ''Yeah right, whatever, Dad.''

He closed her door and went downstairs. Jenna was waiting for him at the bottom of the steps.

''She caught him kissing another girl at school tonight,'' he explained. ''He still wanted to go, but apparently she told him to take a hike.''

''Jerk,'' Jenna said.

''Exactly.''

Jenna looked up the steps. ''Want me to try to talk to her?''

''Nah, I think we'd better just leave her alone.'' Grant put his hand around her shoulders. ''Come on. Let's have dinner.''

Jenna glanced up the stairs one last time. ''Poor baby,'' she said softly. ''I know how much this hurts.''

He kissed her cheek. ''Don't we all?''

The following afternoon, Hannah stood on the front porch dressed in old sweatpants and one of her dad's sweatshirts. She hadn't even taken a shower today. She was going for total grunge and was feeling the part.

''You sure you don't want to come with us?'' her dad asked.

''Dad, I don't want to go to the recital.'' This afternoon was Becka's violin recital, but Hannah couldn't go. Not when she was supposed to be getting ready to go to the dance with Mark. Not when Brittany Anderson was getting ready to go with him at this very moment. She just couldn't. Her sister would just have to understand.

Her dad stood on the sidewalk, obviously trying to make up his mind what to do. She didn't know what she was going to say if he said she had to go. She couldn't possibly go anywhere in public, not looking like this.

"All right," her father relented. "But this is a special exception." He raised a finger. "And after the recital, I'm coming back for you, and we're all going out to dinner."

Hannah knew she wouldn't be up for dinner, but she'd fight with him over that one later. She raised a hand and forced a smile. "You're going to be late. See you later."

He hesitated another moment and then headed down the sidewalk to the car where the girls were already waiting. Jenna and Amy were supposed to go, too, but Amy was home sick with a stomach virus so they weren't going. Of course, it was a wonder her father could go to the recital without goody-two-shoes Jenna. These days they seemed to be stuck together with superglue.

Hannah waited until her father backed out of the driveway and then walked back into the house. She closed the door and leaned against it, not sure what she was going to do. All of her friends were going to the dance, so she didn't have anyone to call. Not that she felt like talking on the phone anyway.

Now that she had gotten over the initial shock of seeing Mark stuffing his tongue down Brittany's throat, she was mostly angry. Still a little hurt, but mostly angry. She wandered into the kitchen, grabbed a cola and went back down the hall. Instead of going upstairs, she veered into her father's den. Maybe she'd borrow one of his movies. Maybe she'd sit here in his cozy chair that her mother had upholstered and watch something really violent like *Apocalypse Now* or something equally gross.

Hannah flopped into her dad's chair and propped up her stockinged feet. She popped open the cola can and gazed at the movies lined up neatly in the entertainment cabinet. They were all in alphabetical order. It was so...*Dad.*

African Queen, Apocalypse Now, Blues Brothers, nothing looked good. Her gaze strayed to a cardboard box beside the entertainment cabinet. She didn't remember seeing it the last time she was in here. It was small, unmarked and taped shut with clear tape.

Hannah got up from the chair to pick up the box. She shook it. There was something hard in it. A book?

She hesitated only a moment and then ripped open the box. She'd tape it shut again later. Maybe it was something her dad wanted to mail and he'd forgotten about it.

To her surprise, there was a videotape in the box. The kind you recorded on yourself. The end was neatly labeled in her dad's handwriting. "Ally."

A tape of her mother? Hannah held the tape in her hand. She should probably ask her dad if it was okay to watch the tape, but why wouldn't it be?

Hannah really missed her mom lately. Things had been going so lousy. First, her father had announced he was marrying Jenna. Hannah liked Jenna well enough, but her father had been spending way too much time with her. Smiling way too much when he talked about her. And then this Mark disaster.

Seeing a tape of her mother was just what Hannah needed to make her feel better.

She slid the tape out of its box. The label on the tape read in her mother's handwriting, "Watch two years after I've been gone." Reading the words gave Hannah goose bumps. It occurred to her that maybe this was private between her mom and dad. Maybe she shouldn't be watching it.

She debated a moment and then popped it into the VCR. She wanted to see her mom.

Hannah sat back in her father's chair and hit Play on the remote. The minute her mother's face appeared on the screen, her eyes filled with tears. Ally Monroe was sitting in this very chair, talking to her dad.

Hannah brushed away her tears, her mother's words suddenly catching her attention. What was her mother talking about? Dating?

Hannah watched the whole tape through twice, and as the minutes passed, her tears dried up and her jaw got tighter. She should have known her father didn't really want to do this to their family. She should have known he was doing the same thing he always did—made plans and then followed through with them.

Hannah rewound the tape, put it back in its case and dropped it into the box. Now what was she going to do? She stared at the still full cola can, chewing on the inside of her cheek.

A minute later she was running upstairs for her sneakers and jacket. She hoped her bike tires had air in them.

Chapter Twelve

Grant walked into the kitchen behind Becka and Maddy, and dropped three bags of groceries onto the table. "Hannah! We're home," he called.

Becka and Maddy were heatedly discussing where they were going for dinner.

"I told you," Grant said, flipping on the kitchen lights. "It's Hannah's choice, now go change if you're going to and let Hannah know we're ready to go when she is."

The two girls left the kitchen, still discussing the attributes of one restaurant's fries over another's.

Grant began to unload the groceries, wondering where Hannah was. He hadn't wanted to leave her home this afternoon while he went to Becka's recital, but he knew he needed to respect his teenager's desire to be alone. He knew how hard it had to be for Hannah to know all of her friends were going to the winter formal tonight and she wasn't.

Grant was not a man who ever thought violence solved a problem, but he was thankful he hadn't seen the ex-boyfriend today. He might not have been able to keep his fingers from around Mark's neck.

As Grant slid a half gallon of orange juice into the refrigerator, he heard a tap on the back door. He glanced up to see Jenna coming in. "Hey," he said, surprised, but pleased to see her. She had intended to go to Becka's recital with them, but Amy hadn't felt well. "Amy better?"

From the look on her face, there was obviously something wrong. She looked as if she had been crying. He hadn't thought Amy was that sick. "Jenna—"

Jenna took a deep breath, trying to stay calm. She wasn't going to cry in front of Grant and she wasn't going to get overly emotional. "Can I speak to you?" she said, her voice sounding odd in her ears. "Privately?"

"Um…yeah, sure." He glanced around the kitchen, then pointed down the hall. "We can close the door to the den."

Jenna followed him into the den and waited while he slid the pocket door shut. She walked to the window and pretended to look out, though she could see nothing but her own reflection in the dark glass.

She looked awful. Some of her hair had slipped from her ponytail, and she had rubbed the makeup off her face.

She closed her fingers over the diamond ring on her left hand. She should have known this was too good to be true. She should have known there was no such thing as fairy tales come true.

She should have known that all princes were really frogs.

"I can't marry you," Jenna said, slipping the ring off her finger.

Grant stood at the door in his gray flannel suit and red tie. He just stared. Blinked. "What?"

She held out the ring and when he didn't immediately take it, she grabbed his hand and pressed it into his palm. "I can't marry you. I won't be a part of 'the plan.'"

"Jenna, what on earth are you talking about?" He looked entirely clueless.

"You know exactly what I'm talking about. I won't be a part of yours and Ally's plan—this neat little package to tie up your life." Tears welled in her eyes and she fought the sob that stuck in her throat.

She hadn't intended to say any more than that, but once she started telling him how she felt, she couldn't stop herself. "You ought to be ashamed of yourself," she accused, shocking not just him, but herself, as well. She couldn't believe she had hollered at him. "How dare you do this to me, to Amy, to your girls. Ask me to marry you because Ally told you to?"

Grant obviously still didn't know exactly what had happened, but she could tell by the crestfallen look on his face that he had some idea now. He knew that she knew what was on Ally's tape.

A part of her wanted to ask him if she could see it. Wanted to demand that she see it. After all, didn't she have the right? But she didn't want to see the tape Hannah had told her about. She felt so betrayed, not just by Grant, but by Ally, too. How could her best friend have schemed this way? How could she have actually told Grant to marry her? How could he have followed through with the whole thing?

"Jenna—"

Grant stepped toward her and she shied from his grasp. If he touched her, she really would fall apart. That or she would smack his face.

"I have to get home. Amy's there alone. I told Mrs. Cannon that I'd be gone only a few minutes."

Grant's face was red. He turned to watch her go as she pushed past him and slid open the pocket door. She could hear Becka and Maddy in the kitchen talking about French fries. She headed for the front door. She couldn't see the girls, not right now.

Jenna grabbed the glass knob of the front door, hoping Grant had the good sense not to follow her...wishing he would anyway. She made it out the door and onto the front porch before she burst into tears. She ran to her car and jumped in and started the engine. As she backed out and put the car into gear, there was still no sign of Grant. He was still standing in the den, probably, glued to the floor in indecision.

Jerk.

* * *

Grant stood in the den staring at the doorway Jenna had just passed through. He was so stunned that he couldn't move. What had just happened here? Apparently, she knew about the videotape, but how?

He turned back to the entertainment center and immediately saw that the box he had packed the tape away in had been opened.

Hannah. Hannah had to have found the videotape. She had told Jenna.

The hard metal of the engagement ring cutting into his palm jolted him into action. As he rounded the staircase, he saw Jenna's headlights as she backed out of the driveway.

Grant *knew* he should have told Jenna about the tape. He really had meant to tell her. But he'd been a coward, so afraid that if he told her, she wouldn't understand. She wouldn't love him, and he needed Jenna to love him. He needed that as much as he had ever needed anything.

Grant took the steps two at a time, the ring still clutched in his hand. "Hannah Jane," he shouted.

Downstairs, Becka and Maddy ceased their chatter in midsentence. If they knew what was good for them, they wouldn't come up the stairs to see what their big sister had done now.

Grant rapped hard on the bedroom door with his knuckles and then pushed in without waiting for Hannah's response.

She was seated at her computer desk, her back to him.

"Dad." She spun around in the chair.

''Shut it off,'' he said quietly but forcefully.

She grabbed the mouse and exited the Internet.

''You showed Jenna the tape.'' It was a statement, not a question. He was so angry. Hurt. Why would Hannah do such a thing? Why would she want to hurt Jenna? Hurt him?

Hannah stared at him, her eyes round. He knew she wasn't used to seeing him like this, barely on the edge of control.

''No. I didn't show her the tape.''

''Hannah, don't lie to me.'' He raised his voice. ''I know Jenna saw the tape. She was just here.'' He squeezed the ring in his hand, fighting the tears that burned the backs of his eyes.

Tears welled in Hannah's eyes. Suddenly she had a horrified look on her face, as if she only now realized she'd made a terrible mistake. Maybe it was the look on his face, the pain he couldn't hide, or maybe she had just come to her senses.

''Oh, Daddy,'' she whispered, bringing her hand to her mouth. Tears slipped down her cheeks. ''Daddy, I did something so wrong. I—''

''You showed Jenna your mother's tape,'' he repeated.

Hannah shook her head. She couldn't even look him in the eye now. ''No,'' she murmured. Fat tears fell from her face to the pale blue carpet. ''I opened the box with the tape in it. I watched it,'' she confessed. ''And then I took my bike to Jenna's and I told her what...'' She started to cry harder. ''I told her what Mom said about you marrying her. I told her you were just doing it because it was all part of a plan, and you liked having a plan.''

Grant looked down at the carpet not knowing who felt worse right now, Jenna or Hannah. His daughter was a good person. He knew she would never have hurt Jenna like this on purpose. He knew she just hadn't been thinking clearly.

''Ah, Hannah,'' he said softly. He slipped Jenna's engagement ring into his suit jacket pocket and went to his daughter. He put his arms around her and pulled her against him, not caring if she rumpled his suit.

''I'm so sorry, Daddy,'' she mumbled into his coat. ''I didn't mean to hurt anyone. I don't know what I was thinking. I was just so upset and I was mad at you because...I don't even know why I was mad at you. And I miss Mommy so much and—''

''Shh,'' Grant soothed, smoothing her silky blond hair. ''It's okay, Hannah. It's going to be all right.''

''What did Jenna say?''

He rubbed her back. ''She gave me back the ring,'' he said quietly.

Hannah broke into a fresh burst of sobs.

Grant didn't know what else to do, but hold her. His own heart was breaking, not just for the ring in his pocket, but for Hannah.

Finally, when she calmed down, he let her go and walked to her dresser to get a box of tissues. He led her to her bed, sat her down and sat beside her.

He dropped the box onto her lap. ''Blow your nose.''

"She gave you back the ring?" Hannah blew her nose. "Oh, Dad, I can't believe I did this."

He handed her another tissue. "I'll fix it. I'll explain it all to Jenna. This is my fault as much as yours." He brushed the hair at his forehead with his hand. "I should have told her about your mother's tape before I ever went out with her."

"I told Jenna that the only reason you were marrying her was because it was the smart thing to do. It's convenient and fits into a nice neat package, but it's not true, is it, Dad?" She looked at him with the earnest face of a child, rather than that of a teen approaching adulthood.

"No," he said quietly, folding his hands. "I asked her to marry me because I love her. I loved your mother, but now she's gone. And even though I still love your mom, I love Jenna. I love her and I want to marry her. I want her to live here with us, and for her and Amy to be a part of our family."

He stared at his hands. "I'm sorry if that makes you unhappy, but honestly, sweetie, you're going to have to get over it." He looked into her red eyes.

Hannah stared at the damp tissue balled in her hands. "I really don't know why I've been acting like this. It's just that I liked Mark so much and I thought he liked me. And you were doing things with Jenna and laughing with her when you used to laugh with me." Tears filled her eyes again.

Grant closed his hand over hers. "Hannah, I understand. It's only natural that you would feel some jealousy toward Jenna. She does take time from you girls, but that's the way it should be. A man my age shouldn't have a life that revolves completely around his children. Shoot, a few months ago you were telling me I needed a life."

Hannah laughed and then sniffed. "So what are we going to do now that I've ruined yours?"

He rose from the bed, unable to resist a smile. "I can tell you what we're going to do. You're going to go downstairs and dig something out of the freezer to feed your sisters and I'm going to Jenna's house. I'm going to get down on my knees and beg her to forgive me."

"Please tell her I'm sorry," Hannah said, getting up. "And...and I'll call her tomorrow and make the apology myself."

Grant reached out and took his daughter by the arm and kissed her forehead. "Don't worry. It's going to be all right between me and Jenna." he said softly. "And if it isn't, it was never meant to be."

When Jenna saw Grant's headlights through the living room curtain, she was tempted to shut out the living room lights, crawl into bed and pull the covers over her head. She didn't want to speak him. She didn't want to see his handsome face. There was nothing to talk about. They couldn't get married. It would never work for a million reasons and she was silly to have ever thought it would.

Instead, she closed Amy's bedroom door and went to the kitchen to make tea.

Grant knocked on the door and walked in. ''Okay if I come in?'' he asked.

She stood in the archway between the living room and kitchen, her hands on her hips. ''Looks like you're already in.''

He closed the door behind him and approached her. ''Jenna, first I want to apologize for letting you walk out of my house like that. I should have stopped you. I was just so shocked.''

''Shocked I knew about the videotape, or shocked I cared?''

He glanced at the floor and then back at her. ''I deserved that.''

She walked over to the couch and sat down, making no attempt to clear a place for him among the newspapers and magazines. ''You shouldn't be angry with Hannah. She didn't make that tape, and she wasn't the one who kept it from me.''

''Well, I am angry with her. That videotape was personal, and she should have realized that when she did watch it. She should have come to me first.'' He scooped up a pile of magazines from the chair beside the couch and dumped them onto the floor, making a seat for himself.

He looked uncharacteristically rumpled and his eyes were red. Her heart gave a little trip. Had Grant been crying? Over her?

But then Jenna stiffened her spine and her resolve. This was not the time to get emotional. He had done a terrible thing, and she was not going to cut him a break. Not one.

"Jenna, I should have told you about the tape the first time I asked you out."

"You asked me out because Ally told you to in that tape, not because you wanted to go out with me."

He nodded. "I *did* ask you out that first time out of some sense of loyalty or something." He met her gaze. "But Jenna, you have to believe me when I tell you, that was as far as it went. I asked you out the second time and the third and the one hundredth because I realized how much I liked you. Because I fell in love with you."

She stared at the pile of papers at his feet. "Hannah said that Ally told you on the tape to marry me."

"What Ally said was that she hoped I would. She said she hoped I would fall in love with you, and you with me, and that's just what happened, Jenna. This wasn't some diabolical plan. All Ally wanted was the two of us to be happy, and apparently she believed we could make each other happy. I guess she knew us better, in a way, than we knew ourselves."

Jenna let her attention drift to a photo on the wall of her and Amy at the beach last summer. "Tell me the truth. You asked me to marry you because it was convenient. Because it fit nicely into one of those plans of yours." She looked at him. "I wouldn't be surprised if you hadn't checked me off some list. Went to the dry cleaners, picked up milk, asked Jenna to marry me."

Grant rubbed his temple. "Jenna, that's not true and you know it. Look, I know I *am* the kind of person who likes control and organization. It's been even more so since Ally died. It was the only way I could keep things together...*appear* to keep things together.'' He paused. ''But this is different. Loving you is different...and you know it. You *know* I love you.''

Jenna had fought tears since Grant walked into the house. Now they welled in her eyes. She wanted to believe him. She loved him so much. But...but she was afraid.

''Please give me another chance,'' he said, reaching for her hand. ''Let me show you how much I love you. How much I need you. Want you.''

She let him hold her hand, but didn't meet his gaze. ''Grant, even if we do love each other, a marriage between us, it...it just wouldn't work. I mean, look at this place.'' She gestured with her other hand. ''Can you really live like this? And can I really deal with the fact that you only own gray suits?''

He frowned. ''I'm not sure I'm getting the gray suit part, but I know what you mean. I can change. Some, at least. I can be more flexible, more spontaneous. I'm willing to change to have you.''

She didn't respond. She wanted so badly to let him take her into his arms and let him kiss away her fears. But she had let her emotions get the best of her and accepted his proposal. For once, she needed to think with her head and not her heart.

''And what about your girls?'' she asked.

''What about them? They love you.''

''Oh, I don't know about that. Hannah didn't seem in too loving a mood when she biked over here a few hours ago to set me straight about why her father was really marrying me.''

''An error in judgment. She was upset about Mark, about the dance, about the fact that, in a way, she was losing me to you.''

''I could never take you away from Hannah. Away from your daughters,'' Jenna said. ''That was never my intention.''

''I know that, and so does Hannah. Like I said, it was just a terrible lapse in judgment. She says she'll talk to you tomorrow and apologize herself.''

Jenna looked away again. ''And what about Amy? She is not the sweet little agreeable young woman she once was. You've seen her. She's moody, she's stubborn. She wants—''

''She wants to spread her wings a little,'' Grant said. ''She wants that independence from you that you've encouraged. That's all. I can live with that. I can adapt. She can come and live with us after we're married or if she wants, we can look into a place like Logan House if that's what she wants. We'll find a way to pay for it.''

Jenna eyed him. ''Don't you start on me. This was where Paul and I—''

''Paul wanted what was best for him,'' Grant interrupted, surprising her with the strength and conviction in his voice. ''That was all he ever wanted and you know it. I want what's best for Amy.''

''And you're suggesting I don't?'' Jenna flared.

''I'm not suggesting anything except that once you and I have settled this between us, we need to talk about Amy, and with Amy.''

Jenna pulled her hand from Grant's to cradle her head. She was so confused. So upset that she couldn't think. Everything Grant said made sense. She did love him, and her heart told her that he really did love her. But it was all too much to process right now, and the ache that had come with Hannah's revelation was still there.

"Grant, I think we need to just take some time apart."

"You mean you'll give me another chance?"

He sounded so hopeful.

"Just give me some time," she repeated. "Let me think."

He got up, sliding his hand into his pocket and pulled out her engagement ring. "You want to keep it?" he said softly. "Just in case?"

It was all she could do to keep from jumping up and throwing her arms around him. Telling him all was forgiven. But she really did need to think. She needed to take the time to balance out her emotions with what was best for her and Amy.

"Keep the ring," she said quietly. "For now."

"Okay," he said steadily. "I'll go, but please, Jenna, know that I love you." His voice caught in his throat. "And know that I would do anything to make this right."

Jenna got up and walked him to the door. "Good night, Grant," she said. She wanted so badly to feel his arms securely around her, his voice in her ear telling her everything was going to be all right. Instead, she let him out the door and then locked it behind him, praying tomorrow she would see things in a better light.

All the following week Jenna avoided Grant. At school, she avoided him in the hallway, and when he called to see how she was doing, she only talked about his girls or Amy. Never about them or about the ring he was still carrying in his suit pocket for all she knew. She just didn't know what to do. She wasn't sure she could trust herself. Now that she had calmed down about the whole videotape thing, she knew that what Grant had said was true. He might have asked her out out of a sense of obligation to Ally, but not even he could fall in love to tie things into a neat little package.

And he *did* love her, so what was holding her back?

It was Amy. Amy had been so unhappy all week. She had even complained about work, saying she didn't like sweeping anymore. She had always loved sweeping the long hallways at school; she'd always loved seeing all of the children.

Sunday morning, Jenna got up bright and early. Next week was Thanksgiving and she thought she and Amy could pull out the Christmas decorations after church. They never put Christmas decorations up until after Thanksgiving, but they could go through the boxes. Amy loved Christmas and all it entailed, and Jenna always enjoyed "doing it up" for her.

Jenna drank a cup of tea and ate a scone, waiting for Amy to get up. It was strange she wasn't up yet. She had always been an early riser. Jenna looked at the kitchen clock. Seven-thirty.

Wondering if Amy might not be feeling well, she went down the hall and opened her bedroom door. The bed was rumpled, but no Amy.

That was strange. She hadn't heard her in the bathroom. She ducked back down the hall. The bathroom was empty.

Where was she?

"Amy!" Jenna called. She checked the front door and to her surprise it was unlocked. It had been locked when she had gone to bed; she had checked it. She went out into the front yard in her pj's and slippers. "Amy?"

Jenna tried to calm the fear that knotted in her stomach. Where was Amy? She had been in her bed last night when Jenna had gone to bed. She'd checked on her.

Jenna went next door to Mrs. Cannon's. Her elderly neighbor had always been a late sleeper, so she didn't want to wake her. The front door was still locked and the Sunday paper was still on the front step. Amy couldn't be there.

Jenna ran back across the lawn. Her breath made big puffs of frost in the air. She tried not to panic as she ran into the house and onto the back porch. Through the paneled glass, she could see the whole garden. No Amy there, either.

Jenna had to call someone. She needed help. But who? The police? No, not yet. There was only one other person she could call. The only one who would understand. She grabbed the phone.

Chapter Thirteen

Grant arrived at Jenna's house in less than ten minutes. Wearing a pair of sweatpants with a hole in the knee and a paint-stained sweatshirt, he strode forcefully into her living room. He didn't even look as if he'd had a shower. Grant's hair was uncharacteristically uncombed and he hadn't shaved.

Grant had come like this without question or hesitation because she needed him. Seeing him here made her realize how natural it had been for her to call him—just as if he were upstairs instead of living in another household.

Jenna was still in her pajamas that had the dancing teapots on them, but if he noticed, he didn't say anything. "You checked next door?" he asked, in a take-command voice.

"Mrs. Cannon is still asleep. She didn't answer her

phone, but she always sleeps late. I know Amy isn't there."

"Okay, where else would she go?" He grabbed the phone, a phonebook and a pad of paper and pen off the counter.

"I don't know." Jenna tried to stay calm, despite the pounding in her ears. Waiting for Grant, a million possibilities of where Amy could be had run through her head. None good. Just having Grant here made her feel better. And having him here made her realize just how much she needed him. She needed him to share not just the good things in life, but the bad things, too.

"She's still going on about Jeffery," Jenna said. "I called Logan House and talked to the director. She said Amy wasn't there but that she would talk to Jeffery and call me back if he knows anything."

Jenna had discovered Amy missing almost twenty minutes ago, and since then she'd managed to do nothing but make a couple of calls and flail her arms, yelling for Amy in the obviously empty house. Grant had been here less than a minute, and he was beginning to make notes on a notepad.

He was doing something positive.

"Okay, where else could she be? Think," Grant said gently, leading her to the couch. He sat on a big pile of newspapers, pulling her down next to him. She stared at his sneakers that were untied.

"I'll call the school," he said. "Barney will be there on a Sunday morning. Maybe she went there, thinking it was a workday. How about the bowling alley?''

''On a Sunday morning?'' Jenna asked. ''It's not open.''

''Does Amy know that?'' He jotted on the pad of paper. ''There must be maintenance staff. I'll call the church office, too. Maybe she went to church without you. Got confused about what time it was. How about girlfriends?''

Jenna twisted her hands on her lap. ''Not really. There's Alison Lutty. We can try her house. Amy always liked Mrs. Lutty's French toast. You know how she is with syrup.''

''Good. That's the way to think,'' he encouraged.

Trying not to cry, Jenna looked into his dark-brown eyes. ''Oh, Grant, what if she's lost? What if someone—''

He grabbed one of her hands firmly. ''Don't worry. We'll find her. Now think. Where would she go?''

The phone Grant held rang, practically scaring Jenna out of her pants. She grabbed it from his hand. ''H...Hello.''

''Jenna?'' a woman's voice came over the phone line. Jenna gripped the cordless phone. ''Yes?''

''This is Madison at Logan House.''

''Jeffery knows where Amy is?'' Jenna said anxiously.

Madison lowered her voice. ''I've just discovered we have an early morning visitor here, after all. I found her sitting on the back porch holding our Sunday paper. Not even Jeffery knew she was here, although he has confessed that he invited her to come for breakfast *sometime.*''

''Amy,'' Jenna managed with a squeak. ''Amy's there and she's all right?''

Madison chuckled. ''She's just fine. She walked all the way here on her own, apparently. She's helping make breakfast right now,'' Madison continued. ''I think she's the egg beater.''

Jenna pressed her hand to her chest. ''She's all right,'' she mouthed to Grant. ''I...I'll come right over for her just as soon as I get dressed,'' Jenna said into the phone.

''No need to hurry. She might as well stay for breakfast.''

Jenna cradled the phone, her relief overwhelming. ''Thank you so much.'' She hung up and looked to Grant. ''She's at Logan House. Apparently Jeffery invited her for breakfast sometime and Amy decided today was the day.'' She managed a weak smile.

Grant grinned. ''I told you she was all right. Get dressed, and I'll drive you over.''

Jenna got up, running a hand over her pajamas, suddenly self-conscious. She knew she must have bed-head. And she wasn't wearing a stitch of makeup. ''Oh, gosh. I'm a mess. I'm so embarrassed for you to see me like this.''

He was still smiling as he kissed her gently on the mouth. ''I think you're pretty sexy in those dancing teacups. Now, go on.'' He patted her playfully on the bottom, and she hurried down the hall.

* * *

Madison greeted her on the front steps of the community house. It was another big rambling Victorian house, much like Grant's home.

"Thank you so much for calling," Jenna said as she hurried up the steps. "Amy's never done this before. I don't know what's gotten into her lately."

Grant followed her up the porch steps.

"It's quite all right. Amy is such a nice young woman. So full of life." Madison smiled. "And so independent. You've done a wonderful job raising her."

Jenna smiled. "Thank you."

Madison hesitated as if she wanted to say something else. "Listen, Jenna, I don't want to put my nose in where it doesn't belong, but Amy has expressed a pretty strong desire to join our family here."

Jenna halted on the porch and glanced behind her to Grant for support. He came to her side to take her hand as if they were together still. A couple still.

"We don't have to talk about it right now but..." The woman hesitated. "I think you should honestly consider her request."

"Oh, no," Jenna said. "Amy is no problem. Really."

Madison paused again. "Of course, she isn't a problem for you. What I meant was that perhaps living with *you* is not what *Amy* wants."

Jenna stared at the house director, not sure what to say. She didn't want to be rude, but how could this total stranger offer an opinion on her relationship with Amy?

"Listen, let's go see Amy, and then maybe you'd like to take a look around. We can make an appointment to talk," Madison suggested. "I think you'll find that Logan House is a wonderful place where Amy might be able to practice that independence you've instilled in her."

Grant squeezed her hand. "It might be a good idea," he offered gently. "Just to hear about the program."

Jenna looked at Madison. "Can I see Amy now?"

"Sure, right this way."

Madison led them into the house, toward the back. Before they reached the kitchen, Jenna could hear others with Down's syndrome talking and laughing. She could hear Amy laughing.

Jenna walked into the kitchen and found six residents and Amy just sitting down to eat at a big table. Jeffery was beside Amy.

"Hi, Jenna. Hi, Grant. These are my friends," Amy said, grinning. "Want some pancakes?"

She looked as happy as Jenna had seen her in months.

Jenna crawled on her hands and knees along the flower bed, dragging a small basket behind her. It was late to dig up her flower bulbs, but luckily the ground was still not frozen. She dug into the cold dirt with her trowel in search of another clump of bulbs. She had always found that gardening work soothed her. Especially when she had a lot on her mind.

Thanksgiving had passed quietly the past weekend. She and Amy had worked at a mission on Thanksgiving Day and shared in a meal with all of the volunteers afterward. Grant and the girls had been there, too, which had been nice. No pressure.

Grant had been so wonderful all week. So understanding. He was trying so hard to be patient with her and give her the time she asked for.

She missed him so much.

Once Jenna had Amy home safe, and she thought about her automatic response in calling Grant, she realized the impact of what calling him really meant. She hadn't needed to call Grant. She could have found Amy on her own. The truth was that she had called Grant because she saw him as her partner. She called him because that was what partners did. They supported each other; they were there for each other.

Truth was, she knew that Ally's tape really wasn't an issue in their relationship. She wished Grant had told her about it to begin with...but then she wondered if he was right. If she had known about the video, she might never have gone out with him. And if she hadn't, would they ever have fallen in love?

Jenna feared that she had reacted the way she had about the tape to cover her own insecurities, her own fears. Her worry over Grant's little idiosyncrasies, the upset over the tape, it all masked a bigger issue. Jenna was afraid. She was afraid to marry Grant and live happily ever after.

And seeing Amy so happy at the kitchen table in Logan House had brought yet another shock of cold, hard reality to Jenna. She had been relying on Amy for a long time, maybe more than Amy had been relying on her. And her dependency on Amy had gotten in the way of her relationship with Grant, probably with Paul, too.

This morning, Jenna and Amy had had a long talk. Amy really wanted to try living at Logan House. Not because of Jeffery, but because she wanted to live on her own. She wanted to rely less on Jenna and more on herself.

How could Jenna deny her sister that opportunity? Today Jenna promised Amy that she would make an appointment with Madison this week. Together the three of them would sit down and talk about Amy joining the Logan House family.

So where did that leave her with Grant? She wasn't sure, but she knew she needed to talk this out with him.

Jenna stood up and brushed the dirt from her hands. She sat on the stone bench in the winter garden and punched in his number on the cordless phone. All she got was the answering machine.

She considered not leaving a message. It would be dinnertime soon. He needed to feed the kids, make sure homework was done and get everyone into bed at a reasonable time. She could talk to him tomorrow, if not in school, then tomorrow night on the phone.

When the answering machine beeped, Jenna paused. "Hey, you," she said softly. "I...I just wanted to tell you that…that I miss you. Let's talk tomorrow. Good night."

Jenna hung up the phone and began to gather her gardening tools. She'd go in, get cleaned up and have dinner with Amy. There was already homemade soup simmering on the back of the stove. Tomorrow, she would talk to Grant. Tomorrow, she would try to make things right between them.

"No, Tiffany. I'm sorry. You can't bring your pony for show-and-tell," Jenna told one of her students. "Where would we keep her during reading time?" She ushered the pigtailed student to an activity table.

"Jerome, please do not eat the beads. If you eat the beads, no one else will be able to make a necklace."

Jenna checked off the name of each student in her attendance book as he or she arrived, and then directed each toward an activity table. Once Grant read the morning announcements, she would seat her students in the tiny bleachers she'd had made, and they would begin their morning routine. The pledge, a review of the date of the day, the weather outside and then they would move on to the letter of the week.

Jenna had hoped she could speak with Grant this morning. She knew they would need more time to talk than what could be stolen as buses were arriving, but now that she realized she had been shortchanging herself and Grant, she really needed to talk with him. She needed him to know that she, like Hannah, had exercised an error in judgment. She wanted to make their relationship work. She wanted to marry him.

"Good morning, students," came Grant's voice over the loudspeaker.

Jenna's class instantly became quiet. Jenna was notorious for being a fun teacher, but also notorious for having well-behaved students.

"Before I read this morning's quote of the day, I'd like to make a special announcement."

Jenna walked to her desk to put down her attendance book. What was up with Grant this morning? He never strayed from his morning routine. Never. First a quote, then the daily announcements.

"Actually, I have a question. This isn't for you students, but it's one I think is important to hear."

Jenna was so surprised by Grant's strange speech that she turned to face the intercom near the door.

"Miss Cartwright, would you do me the honor of being my wife?"

Jenna's eyes widened in shock. Had she just heard what she thought she'd heard?

Her students burst into muffled giggles. As she turned to the class, she could see them whispering behind their hands. Jenna's assistant, Martha, stood at the other end of the classroom grinning at Jenna.

There was a pause and the crackle of static over the intercom. "A yes right about now would be good," Grant said.

Jenna realized he was expecting an answer this minute. She stood a moment in indecision. Should she walk down to the office? Or should she run?

She was giddy with surprise. She couldn't believe Grant had done such a thing. Asked her to marry him over the intercom? It was so not Grant.

Jenna leaned toward the intercom and pushed the blue button that not only would return a message to the office, but also would broadcast it to the entire school.

"Yes, Dr. Monroe, I'll marry you."

Martha began to clap, and Jenna's students jumped out of their little multicolored chairs, cheering.

Jenna looked to Martha. "Be right back," she mouthed.

As Jenna headed down the hall toward the office, she heard Grant go on with announcements. He read a quote from Thomas Paine and reminded all sixth graders that he needed their permission slips to go see *The Nutcraker,* by the end of the week.

Jenna turned the corner, and spotted Grant coming from the main office toward her. They met halfway down the hall and she threw herself into his arms. "I'm so sorry," she said. "I've been so foolish."

Grant looked up the hall one way and down the other, grabbed her arm and dragged her into the ladies' room.

Jenna couldn't stop giggling. "Grant Monroe! You surprise me. First you ask me to marry you over the intercom—"

"So you wouldn't dare say no," he said.

"And then you drag me into the ladies' room? The Grant Monroe I know wouldn't be caught dead in a ladies' room—"

"So I can kiss you," he murmured.

Their mouths met hungrily. It had been too long.

"I love you, Jenna," he murmured, tearing himself from her mouth. "Marry me, and I swear I'll make you happy."

Of course she would marry him. She grabbed his red tie and pulled him close to kiss him again.

"Marry me," he whispered against her lips. "And I promise I'll keep you guessing. I promise our life will never be predictable. I'll even leave some dirty clothes on the floor, just to keep you guessing."

She kissed him again. "Keep your dirty clothes," she teased, "and it's a deal."

A moment later Jenna and Grant walked out of the ladies' room. Jenna was flustered, her ponytail askew. As they stepped out the swinging door that read Ladies, she turned to adjust Grant's tie.

To their surprise, the hallway was filled with students and teachers, all clapping. Hand in hand, Jenna and Grant walked the gauntlet, and Jenna knew in her heart she'd found her prince.

Epilogue

Two and a Half Years Later

"Mrs. Monroe, will you come play Frisbee?" One of Jenna's kindergarten students ran across the beach, kicking sand. "Please?"

Jenna laughed as she scooped up balls and Frisbees the children had left strewn on the shore. Becka tagged behind her, carrying a beach bag to toss them into. "Give me another five minutes to clean, and I'll be down," she told her student.

Today was Starfish Academy's annual Last Day of School Picnic. On a stretch of beach on the bay side, she and Grant and several other teachers and parents had set up a picnic area. They had served hot dogs and hamburgers from the grill, plenty of potato salad and chips and, of course, the traditional steamed clams. Now, while adults cleaned up, the children ran along the beach, some wading in the calm waters, while others played various games. Up the beach, the new high school graduate, Hannah, and her boyfriend, Jared, were setting up a volleyball net while Maddy directed.

Jenna's student jogged off, and Jenna turned to Becka, dropping a small beach ball into the bag. "I think that's it for the moment. Why don't you go play with the others?"

"Can I take Rose down to the water?"

"Where is she?" Jenna wore sunglasses, but she still had to shade her eyes to glance down the beach.

"Dad has her. Here they come. I think they went to the car to change her diaper."

Jenna turned east to the dunes to see Grant headed toward them, one-year-old baby Rose in one arm, a large diaper bag on the other.

"Just her toes in the water," Jenna warned Becka.

Of all of the children, Becka was the one who had truly taken to big sisterhood. She adored Rose and was actually a lifesaver. With working, a husband and four children, Jenna could easily have been overwhelmed at times. But all of the girls and Grant pitched in so much, that life ran pretty smoothly.

"Hey," Jenna called to Grant, grinning. She still couldn't get over how lucky she was, how happy she was. She and Grant had certainly had their share of bumps and bruises since their wedding, but those little snags just seemed to make their relationship even stronger. If possible, Jenna thought she loved Grant more now than she had the day she said "I do" more than two years ago.

"Hey," Grant answered, smiling back. His face was suntanned, his hair slightly wavy from the wind and salt air. From behind the dark sunglasses, his brown eyes sparkled.

Jenna took Rose from his hands and the baby laughed and wiggled. She passed her to Becka.

"I know, just her feet," Becka said.

Standing side-by-side, Jenna and Grant watched Becka wade through the soft sand, carrying her baby sister on her hip. "Where are the girls?" Grant asked, casually slipping his arm around Jenna's waist.

"Let's see, Maddy, Hannah and 'the new man' are setting up the volleyball nets. Amy and Jeffery, and I think half of Logan House, are down by the water running races with the students and..." She turned to him. "This girl is right here with you."

Grant slipped his other hand around her waist and brought his mouth to hers. It was a slow, sensual kiss that made her tingle right to her bare, sandy toes.

"You think that's appropriate, Principal Monroe, kissing a teacher right here in the open on the beach?" she teased.

"I think it's entirely appropriate for children to see a married couple expressing their affection for each other." He ran his hand over her bottom, and she smacked it away. "Not that anyone is paying any attention to us. They're having too good a time on the school picnic that their teacher organized."

"That we *all* organized," she corrected.

He kept his arms around her. ''So, you going to save me a seat beside you at the campfire tonight?''

''Depends,'' she chuckled. ''Can you keep your hands off me?''

He gave her that boyish grin that she loved. ''Can't promise.''

''Then it's a deal.'' She lifted on her toes in the soft sand and kissed him. ''I love you,'' she murmured. ''Thank you.''

''For what?'' He brushed the hair from her face that caught on the bay breeze.

''I don't know. For rescuing me from a life of spinsterhood.''

''Then I guess I should thank you for rescuing me, too. I was working myself into a pretty pathetic little life with my labeled freezer foods and red ties.''

She laughed, smoothing his polo shirt. ''Guess we really should thank Ally,'' she murmured, a bittersweet lump catching in her throat. ''Perhaps if it wasn't for her and that tape...''

''We'd never have been this happy,'' he finished for her. ''Now come on.'' He grabbed her hand. ''Let's show those kids how to play some serious volleyball.''

* * * * *

HARLEQUIN MOTHER'S DAY CONTEST 2216
OFFICIAL RULES
NO PURCHASE NECESSARY TO ENTER

Two ways to enter:

- **Via The Internet:** Log on to the Harlequin romance website (www.eHarlequin.com) anytime beginning 12:01 a.m. E.S.T., January 1, 2002 through 11:59 p.m. E.S.T., April 1, 2002 and follow the directions displayed on-line to enter your name, address (including zip code), e-mail address and in 100 words or fewer, describe how your mother helped with the romance in your life.

- **Via Mail:** Handprint (or type) on an 8 1/2" x 11" plain piece of paper, your name, address (including zip code) and e-mail address (if you have one), and in 100 words or fewer, describe how your mother helped with the romance in your life. Mail your entry via first-class mail to: Harlequin Mother's Day Contest 2216, (in the U.S.) P.O. Box 9076, Buffalo, NY 14269-9076; (in Canada) P.O. Box 637, Fort Erie, Ontario, Canada L2A 5X3.

For eligibility, entries must be submitted either through a completed Internet transmission or postmarked no later than 11:59 p.m. E.S.T., April 1, 2002 (mail-in entries must be received by April 9, 2002). Limit one entry per person, household address and e-mail address. On-line and/or mailed entries received from persons residing in geographic areas in which entry is not permissible will be disqualified.

Entries will be judged by a panel of judges, consisting of members of the Harlequin editorial, marketing and public relations staff using the following criteria:

- Originality - 50%
- Emotional Appeal - 25%
- Sincerity - 25%

In the event of a tie, duplicate prizes will be awarded. Decisions of the judges are final.

Prize: A 6-night/7-day stay for two at the Inter-Continental San Juan Resort & Casino, including round-trip coach air transportation from gateway airport nearest winner's home (approximate retail value: $4,000). Prize includes breakfast daily and a mother and daughter day of beauty at the beachfront hotel's spa. Prize consists of only those items listed as part of the prize. Prize is valued in U.S. currency.

All entries become the property of Torstar Corp. and will not be returned. No responsibility is assumed for lost, late, illegible, incomplete, inaccurate, non-delivered or misdirected mail or misdirected e-mail, for technical, hardware or software failures of any kind, lost or unavailable network connections, or failed, incomplete, garbled or delayed computer transmission or any human error which may occur in the receipt or processing of the entries in this Contest.

Contest open only to residents of the U.S. (except Colorado) and Canada, who are 18 years of age or older and is void wherever prohibited by law; all applicable laws and regulations apply. Any litigation within the Province of Quebec respecting the conduct or organization of a publicity contest may be submitted to the Régie des alcools, des courses et des jeux for a ruling. Any litigation respecting the awarding of a prize may be submitted to the Régie des alcools, des courses et des jeux only for the purpose of helping the parties reach a settlement. Employees and immediate family members of Torstar Corp. and D.L. Blair, Inc., their affiliates, subsidiaries and all other agencies, entities and persons connected with the use, marketing or conduct of this Contest are not eligible to enter. Taxes on prize are the sole responsibility of winner. Acceptance of any prize offered constitutes permission to use winner's name, photograph or other likeness for the purposes of advertising, trade and promotion on behalf of Torstar Corp., its affiliates and subsidiaries without further compensation to the winner, unless prohibited by law.

Winner will be determined no later than April 15, 2002 and be notified by mail. Winner will be required to sign and return an Affidavit of Eligibility form within 15 days after winner notification. Non-compliance within that time period may result in disqualification and an alternate winner may be selected. Winner of trip must execute a Release of Liability prior to ticketing and must possess required travel documents (e.g. Passport, photo ID) where applicable. Travel must be completed within 12 months of selection and is subject to traveling companion completing and returning a Release of Liability prior to travel; and hotel and flight accommodations availability. Certain restrictions and blackout dates may apply. No substitution of prize permitted by winner. Torstar Corp. and D.L. Blair, Inc., their parents, affiliates, and subsidiaries are not responsible for errors in printing or electronic presentation of Contest, or entries. In the event of printing or other errors which may result in unintended prize values or duplication of prizes, all affected entries shall be null and void. If for any reason the Internet portion of the Contest is not capable of running as planned, including infection by computer virus, bugs, tampering, unauthorized intervention, fraud, technical failures, or any other causes beyond the control of Torstar Corp. which corrupt or affect the administration, secrecy, fairness, integrity or proper conduct of the Contest, Torstar Corp. reserves the right, at its sole discretion, to disqualify any individual who tampers with the entry process and to cancel, terminate, modify or suspend the Contest or the Internet portion thereof. In the event the Internet portion must be terminated a notice will be posted on the website and all entries received prior to termination will be judged in accordance with these rules. In the event of a dispute regarding an on-line entry, the entry will be deemed submitted by the authorized holder of the e-mail account submitted at the time of entry. Authorized account holder is defined as the natural person who is assigned to an e-mail address by an Internet access provider, on-line service provider or other organization that is responsible for arranging e-mail address for the domain associated with the submitted e-mail address. Torstar Corp. and/or D.L. Blair Inc. assumes no responsibility for any computer injury or damage related to or resulting from accessing and/or downloading any sweepstakes material. Rules are subject to any requirements/limitations imposed by the FCC. **Purchase or acceptance of a product offer does not improve your chances of winning.**

For winner's name (available after May 1, 2002), send a self-addressed, stamped envelope to: Harlequin Mother's Day Contest Winners 2216, P.O. Box 4200 Blair, NE 68009-4200 or you may access the www.eHarlequin.com Web site through June 3, 2002.

Contest sponsored by Torstar Corp., P.O. Box 9042, Buffalo, NY 14269-9042.